"Are you saying you feel nothing for me?" Gabe asked.

Laurie looked away. "No," she said quietly, heading for the door.

She never got there. He reached out and seized her wrist, pulling her against him. "Prove it."

She came into his arms stiffly, determined to hide the depth of her desire for him, but her resolution ended the moment his lips touched her skin. He kissed her gently, brushing his lips against her temple in an almost reverent caress, cherishing her more than words could say.

Raw fire coursed through her body. "We can't do this," she said, trying to keep her wits about her.

His lips pressed against her brow, and she felt them turn into a smile. "Can't? I haven't been able to sleep nights thinking about the different ways we can. . . ."

WHAT ARE *LOVESWEPT* ROMANCES?

They are stories of true romance and touching emotion. We believe those two very important ingredients are constants in our highly sensual and very believable stories in the LOVE-SWEPT line. Our goal is to give you, the reader, stories of consistently high quality that may sometimes make you laugh, sometimes make you cry, but are always fresh and creative and contain many delightful surprises within their pages.

Most romance fans read an enormous number of books. Those they truly love, they keep. Others may be traded with friends and soon forgotten. We hope that each LOVESWEPT romance will be a treasure—a "keeper." We will always try to publish

LOVE STORIES YOU'LL NEVER FORGET
BY AUTHORS YOU'LL ALWAYS REMEMBER

The Editors

Loveswept ® 705

TAMING THE PIRATE

RUTH OWEN

BANTAM BOOKS

NEW YORK · TORONTO · LONDON · SYDNEY · AUCKLAND

TAMING THE PIRATE

A Bantam Book / August 1994

If you would be interested in receiving protective vinyl covers for your
Loveswept books, please write to this address for information:

Loveswept
Bantam Books
P.O. Box 985
Hicksville, NY 11802

ISBN 0-553-44427-1

Published simultaneously in the United States and Canada

Bantam Books are published by Bantam Books, a division of Bantam Dou-
bleday Dell Publishing Group, Inc. Its trademark, consisting of the words
"Bantam Books" and the portrayal of a rooster, is Registered in U.S.
Patent and Trademark Office and in other countries. Marca Registrada.
Bantam Books, 1540 Broadway, New York, New York 10036.

PRINTED IN THE UNITED STATES OF AMERICA

OPM   0 9 8 7 6 5 4 3 2 1

To my godson
Hudson Brainerd,
a hero
in the making

PROLOGUE

The sound of wings.

Laurie glanced up, holding her breath in wonder as she watched the flight of angels rise into the midnight sky. Their enormous wings beat the air with hurricane force, sending soft feathers swirling down around her face and shoulders, brushing like a lover's touch against her naked skin. Soft feathers, silk feathers—feathers as dark as murder and as bright as hope. She held up her hands like a child in the rain, laughing in amazement and joy.

More feathers fell. They whirled around her faster and faster, wrapping her in a maelstrom of churning air and color. Then things changed. They stiffened and stung her unprotected skin like hard rain, hurting her. One sharp edge gashed her cheek. Panicked, she threw her hands over her eyes, only to have her soft palms cut by the sharp, rigid spines.

Tornado winds roared by her face. She couldn't

breathe. Hardening feathers lashed her body like a whip, cutting deep gashes into her back and legs. She screamed, but no one heard her. Glass-sharp feathers danced around her like demon knives, stabbing her, cutting her, killing her . . .

"No!" Laurie screamed, bolting upright in her bed. She sat in the darkness, gulping air, searching the shadows for feathers and wings. But the shadows were empty, and the only sounds she heard were the muffled hum of the traffic in the street below her window, and the frantic beat of her own heart.

Gradually the terror of the dream subsided. Her heart stopped pounding, her breathing slowed. She pulled the sweat-dampened sheets away from her cotton sleep-shirt, and swung her legs over the edge of the bed, resting her feet on the bare wooden floorboards. "Damn," she muttered, feeling the familiar ache of helplessness well up inside her. "Not again."

Wearily Laurie got up from the bed and padded silently down the narrow hallway of her newly rented apartment, until she reached the door at the end. She knew she was being overly cautious—nightmares, even terrifying ones, were no threat to Adam. Still, she checked. She put her ear to the wood, measuring the silence with a practiced ear, then slowly pushed the door open.

Soft moonlight poured into the room, glazing the small figure in the bed with a faint, gentle luster. Surrounded by a chaos of covers, books, and toys, Adam slept peacefully, hugging his plastic commandos and his favorite stuffed bunny to his chest. His hushed, steady breathing was the only sound that broke the silence.

Relieved, she walked over and knelt beside him, tenderly brushing a stray strand of coal-black hair from his forehead. She treasured the intimate moment, knowing her very grown-up six-year-old would never have tolerated such a motherly gesture if he were awake. Adam had the independence of a lion cub —an independence she'd sensed in him since the first moment she'd held him in her arms. *Was it only six years ago? It seemed like six lifetimes.*

She gazed at her son, and felt peace and love wash away the terror in her heart. As long as Adam was safe, nothing else mattered. Nothing. Tomorrow she would find him a reliable sitter and look for a job. They would build a new life for themselves in this big, sprawling city of Miami—as Laurie Palmer, single mother, and her son Adam. She tucked the covers gently around his chin, and let herself believe for a moment that she and Adam were really just an ordinary, unremarkable woman and her ordinary, unremarkable son. It was a wonderful fantasy, but short-lived. She spotted a copy of Dante's *Inferno* tucked under Adam's pillow.

The sound of wings.

She stood abruptly, unintentionally jostling the bed so hard that it woke Adam. He yawned widely and blinked up at her, barely awake. "Mommy?"

"Go to sleep, darling," she said, fighting to keep the anguish out of her voice. "It was only a dream."

Apparently satisfied, he snuggled deeper into the

covers, falling fast asleep again in less than a minute. Laurie listened to his breathing for a moment, then tiptoed out of the room, closing the door behind her. She leaned against it, and brushed silent tears from her cheeks. She wanted to scream, to yell out her fear and anger until someone, anyone listened to her. But all the people she'd trusted had betrayed her. There was no one she could turn to for help, no one at all.

Laurie wrapped her arms around her slight body, feeling a bone-deep chill that had nothing to do with the temperature. It had only been a nightmare, but the threat behind it was very real. She could pretend all she wanted, but she and Adam would never be able to live normal lives.

Not as long as the security "angels" of TechniKon Industries were after them.

ONE

El Diablo was broken again. Gabe Ramirez lay sprawled on his back on the linoleum floor of his office and looked up into the mechanical guts of his ancient air-conditioning unit, feeling outmaneuvered. *Diablo* had an uncanny knack of breaking down only on the hottest Miami days, and this morning was no exception. Though it was still only April, the weatherman predicted that the mercury would hit one hundred degrees by afternoon. Judging from the hot, humid air that blew in through his wide open windows, Gabe believed the weatherman was being optimistic.

He twisted a strategic-looking valve, and barked a sharp Cuban curse when the knob came off in his hand. Damn! he was sick of this thing. He pushed himself out from under the unit and looked around his small, modestly furnished storefront office, feeling sick of it as well. For two years he'd run his investigation business out of this place, helping his friends and neighbors carve little victories out of a legal system that was heavily weighted against the average man. He made a comfortable living, but it paled to insignificance beside his high-flying past. Sometimes he couldn't help wondering what would have happened if he'd chosen differently, if he'd said yes to the tainted offer instead of no.

You still have your honor, his mind whispered.

But a man couldn't bank on his honor. And he sure as hell couldn't use it to repair a demonic air conditioner. Smiling grimly, he rolled up the sleeves of his cotton shirt—a ready-to-wear brand rather than the tailored variety he'd worn in the old days—and shoved his lean, powerful body under the unit again, determined to fix *El Diablo* or die in the attempt. He had just located the broken Freon line when Yoli rushed in, yelling at the top of her lungs.

"I've found her!"

Startled, Gabe sat up, and conked his head on the metal underbelly. Cursing silently he pulled himself out and looked daggers at his secretary. "Found who?" he asked as he rubbed his smarting forehead.

"Her," Yoli said, tossing her frizzy yellow curls in triumph. "The *Empress.*"

Gabe's hand stilled midrub. He was working three missing persons cases at the moment, and none of them involved royalty. Not for the first time, he wished he'd never given in to the impulse to hire the batty blonde, even if she had needed the job. "Yoli," he said with long-suffering patience, "we are not looking for an empress."

"We aren't, but you are," she replied. "Of course, she isn't the Empress yet. She's the Queen of Swords. But she'll become the Empress after you fall in love with her."

"After I fall . . ." Gabe repeated, his words dwindling into silence. Yoli had really gone off the deep end this time. He ran his hand over his face, wondering if her sudden madness would prevent her from typing that twenty-page report he needed so badly, when a thought struck him. "You aren't talking about those damn cards again, are you?"

Yoli clutched the quartz crystal hanging from a silver chain around her neck. "You shouldn't make fun of the Tarot. The cards never lie."

Gabe's mood hadn't been great when Yoli entered the room, and her announcement did nothing to improve it. Hot and frustrated, he was tempted to tell Yoli exactly what he thought of her Tarot cards, her tea leaves, and all her other physic paraphernalia. He didn't, of course. Yoli's belief in the New Age movement had turned the lonely, timid widow into a lively extrovert. Personally, he thought the whole thing was about as credible as Uncle Carlos's "foolproof" horse-handicapping system, but he kept that opinion to himself. Hoax or not, the change in her was genuine. But that didn't mean *he* believed in this fortune-telling nonsense, and he intended to put a stop to it right now. "Yoli, I have a girlfriend."

"You have several," she stated bluntly, "but no

one you truly care about. And no one who truly cares about you."

That remark hit him a little too close to the bone for comfort. "I'm not looking for a long-term commitment. Besides," he added, flashing her a pirate's grin, "you know my heart belongs to *Dulcinea*."

Yoli's pale brows drew together in a stern frown. She was one of the few women in the city unmoved by Gabe's rakish smile. It was, he had to admit, one of the things he liked best about her. She had a knack for seeing beneath a person's exterior, into their hearts. Besides, she was the only secretary he'd ever had who put up with his odd hours and exacting standards.

When a case gripped him, he became a man possessed, foregoing meals, sleep, and good manners to see it through to the end. It was this same single-minded determination that had gotten him promoted, and then fired, from the Miami police force.

Easygoing Yoli was the ideal secretary for him. She was also crazy as a bedbug.

"Yoli, next time ask those cards something useful. Like how to fix this son-of-a-dog air conditioner." Sighing, he picked up his screwdriver and turned back to *El Diablo*, preparing once more to do battle with his adversary. He lay down and braced his long legs to push himself under the unit, but before he did Yoli cried out and pointed toward the open window.

"There she is. There's the Empress!" she exclaimed.

Gabe groaned aloud, knowing he shouldn't look. His secretary's predictions, though frequent, were never right. Besides, he knew everyone in the Calle Ocho neighborhood of Miami's Little Havana, and all the women under fifty were either married, engaged, or . . . well, not interested in limiting their enterprise by marriage. Still, he was curious to see what kind of woman Yoli's dubious fortune-telling powers had chosen as his perfect mate. *It couldn't hurt to look*, he reasoned silently as he pulled his lean body to its full six feet height and followed Yoli's gaze out the window. *She's probably big as a house, anyway.*

He was wrong. She was as big as *two* houses.

"Carlotta Vazquez?" Gabe said, gaping at his secretary in shock. "But she's . . . married."

Yoli made a sound of profound exasperation. "Not her. The other woman. Near the apartment building steps."

Gabe looked again and spotted a slim, leggy figure standing in the building's shadow. The too-large shirt and shorts she wore hung on her slight frame like rags on a scarecrow. "The scrawny one? *Concho*, Yoli, I could never take her out on the water. A stiff ocean breeze would blow that one away."

The words had barely left his mouth when a young, dark-haired boy ran down the steps of the apartment building and sailed full tilt into the girl's arms. She caught him with ease. Gabe's hawk-sharp eyes narrowed as he automatically read the body language between them, determining beyond a doubt that the boy was her son. "Okay, so she's stronger than she looks," Gabe admitted, "but she's not really my type—"

His words ended abruptly as she stepped out of the shadows and the full force of the sun caught her blonde, shoulder-length hair. It was veined with a copper so wondrously bright it seemed to outshine the sun itself. Gabe leaned toward the open window, his heart pounding in his chest. *No, not copper. Redgold . . .*

Gold. Centuries ago it had lured his ancestors away from their comfortable Spanish haciendas, driving them to risk the treacherous seas and the hangman's noose for its gleaming promise. Dozens had died, or been captured, drowned or worse in their lusty pursuit of treasure. But dozens more had lived and settled their families in the secret island harbors of the lawless Caribbean.

Pirates all, the Ramirez forefathers gradually turned their plundered treasure into legitimate fortunes, eventually becoming one of the richest and most powerful families in Cuba. Castro's takeover had stripped them of most of their wealth and exiled them to America, but the lure of gold remained, as much a part of the Ramirez men as their razor-sharp wits or their glossy black hair.

Gabe had thought himself immune to the family heritage. He'd never lusted after material wealth, not even when he'd traveled in the glittering circles of Miami's social elite. But the gold in the woman's hair stirred his blood in a way he'd never imagined, just as the first doubloon had enticed his many-times greatgrandfather all those years ago.

There was a saying in his family, handed down

through the generations. Once a pirate, always a pirate.

He watched the bright-haired woman and her son walk hand in hand down the street, never taking his eyes off her until she turned a corner and disappeared from his sight. Even then, he continued to stare at the corner, hoping to catch another glimpse of her. He might have watched for her all day, if a muffled laugh behind him hadn't caught his attention. He turned around, and found Yoli studying him, looking entirely too pleased with herself.

Reality doused his passion like a bucket of cold water. Savvy, shrewd, and occasionally ruthless Gabe Ramirez never let anyone get the better of him. He'd built his professional reputation on it. Yet his ozone secretary and a red-haired *chiquita* had just made him behave like a first-class idiot. *¡Válgame Dios!* If this got out he'd never live it down.

He shrugged his shoulders and hunkered back down in front of *El Diablo*, hoping that Yoli would assume he was disinterested and leave. No such luck. Flighty Yoli possessed a steel streak of determination that was every bit as stubborn as his.

"Her name is Laurie Palmer," she said, answering the question he purposely hadn't asked. "The boy is her six-year-old son Adam. She moved into the Perezes' apartment building across the street last week." Then, as if saving the best for last, she raised her left hand and wiggled her fingers. "And she's not wearing a ring."

Gabe scooted back under the air conditioner. "Save your breath, Yoli. I'm not interested."

"Nonsense," his secretary continued, undaunted. "She's perfect for you. She's pretty, exceptionally bright, and has a great sense of humor. Anyway, you need someone in your life. It's been almost two years since—"

"I'm not interested!" Gabe snarled, his harsh words startling her into silence. "And get back to work. I'm not paying you to stand around doing nothing!"

Yoli stiffened. "Well, you don't have to be nasty about it," she stated, and left the room without another word.

After she'd gone Gabe pulled himself out from under the unit and sat on his haunches, feeling guilty. Yoli knew about his whole sordid past, but she never condemned him for it like so many of his so-called friends. She didn't deserve to be yelled at like that. But people rarely get what they deserve, he thought, his lips curving into a cynical smile.

Hot, muggy air blew in through the window, thick and stifling with the growing heat of the day. He wiped the beaded sweat from his brow and gazed around the small, run-down office, feeling the ordinariness of his life tighten around his neck like a noose. Not for the first time he questioned his decision to break with his old life and make a new start. Life in the fast lane hadn't been entirely fulfilling, but at least he had never been bored. He threw down the screwdriver and growled with a soul-deep frustration.

Tonight he would escape. He would take *Dulcinea* to the reef and sit under the stars, letting the rocking waves lull him into forgetfulness. And, just for a moment, he might pretend that someone sat beside him in the starlight, a woman with red-gold hair. But pretending was all it could be, he reminded himself.

For two years his boat *Dulcinea* had been the only long-term woman in his life. And, whatever Yoli or her Tarot cards said, he knew it was better that way.

He remembered all too clearly what had happened the last time he'd fallen for a golden-haired woman.

I need three hands, Laurie determined as she and Adam approached the heavy security door to her apartment building, her arms weighed down with groceries. Logical by nature, she firmly believed that every problem, when studied properly, had a solution. However, she usually came up with something more practical than growing an extra appendage.

"Want some help, lady?" a young voice behind her asked.

She turned and saw a gangly teenage boy walking toward her, smiling broadly. He wore an oversize Miami Heat basketball jersey and loud orange beach shorts with a matching hat turned backward on his head. His deep brown eyes were as guileless as a newborn puppy's.

Laurie sighed in relief, surprised and grateful to discover that chivalry wasn't completely dead. "You're a lifesaver," she said as she handed him one of her bags.

The boy smiled and nodded in acknowledgment. Then, still smiling pleasantly, he took off down the street with her groceries.

"Mommy, he robbed us!" Adam cried as he valiantly ran after the young criminal.

"Adam, no!" Dropping her remaining packages, Laurie sprinted after her young son and caught up with him in a dozen steps. Panicked and winded, she knelt on the sidewalk and wrapped him in a tight bear hug. "Don't *ever* take off like that again."

"But we're losing him!"

Laurie glanced at the traffic speeding by on the street beside her. "The only thing I couldn't bear losing is *you.*"

"Aw, Mom," Adam said, clearly embarrassed by her outburst.

He struggled out of her arms, but he kept a firm grip on her hand, as if some part of him wasn't quite as grown-up as he wanted his mother to believe. Suppressing a smile, Laurie pretended not to notice.

She looked down the street, searching for a glimpse of the thief, but wasn't surprised when she couldn't find a trace of him. More than likely the boy had ducked into an alley or side street—in any case, he was well and truly gone. She could kiss that sack of groceries good-bye.

Sighing, she turned back to her other bag, the one she'd dropped on the sidewalk when she ran after her son. Crushed and mangled vegetables covered the pavement, and an egg yolk slid slowly over the edge of the sidewalk and into the street. Disheartened, she felt a certain kinship with the gooey mess. "Well," she said, trying to smile for Adam's sake, "I guess it's good we like our eggs scrambled. . . ."

The poor joke did nothing to lighten her spirits. As she and her son knelt down to salvage what remained of their groceries, she began to wonder if the whole world hadn't suddenly turned against them.

People brushed by them, hardly sparing a glance in their direction. Some even quickened their pace as they passed. No one offered to help. Laurie looked up at the stony faces, feeling more alone and isolated than she ever had in her life. *Hell*, she thought bleakly, *isn't there someone in this city who gives a damn?*

Adam lifted his head in curiosity and glanced down the street. "Something's going down."

"Going *on*," she said, refusing to let her son's language deteriorate before he even reached the first grade. She heard the commotion too. She craned her neck around, and was surprised to see the young thief walking back toward her, her sack still firmly in his grasp. "What the—?" she began, but the words died in her throat. She caught sight of the man who followed the boy.

He was the kind of man who demanded notice, even on a crowded Miami street. Tall and dark, he moved with an economy of motion that both fascinated and frightened her. The sleeves of his white shirt were rolled up past his elbows, emphasizing the rich color of his skin, and the sinewy length of his forearms. He wasn't muscle-bound, yet he radiated a strength that went beyond mere physical power. The people on the sidewalk stepped aside for him, showing him the deference the citizens of another country might have showed to their king.

Or their conqueror, she thought uneasily.

The unknown man prodded the thief until they came to a stop in front of her. "Jimmy, I believe there's something you want to say to the lady."

His slightly accented baritone spilled through her like warm Cuban rum. Up close, she could see his aristocratic features, the strong, almost arrogant beauty of his face. But it wasn't his looks which drew the lion's share of her attention, it was his partially unbuttoned shirtfront and the tantalizing glimpse of dark chest hair it revealed. Laurie reminded herself that she was far too sensible to be drooling over a man's spectacular build like some love-struck teenybopper. That knowledge didn't make breathing any easier.

Jimmy cleared his throat. "I'm sorry," he said, carefully setting the bag near her feet.

The man behind him gently cuffed the boy's shoulder. "And?"

"And I'll pay for any groceries that got ruined," he added. He looked at her, his expression genuinely contrite. "I really am sorry, lady. I didn't know you were a friend of Gabe's."

Friend? That wasn't the word that leapt to mind when she looked at the devastatingly handsome man. The ones that did, however, made her skin itch from the inside out. She looked down, focusing an unwarranted amount of attention on the returned groceries. "That will be fine."

Jimmy, sensing a reprieve, dashed off down the street before she could get another word out. She watched him go, feeling inexplicably like she'd lost an ally. A deep chuckle brought her out of her musings.

"Jimmy is a good kid, but he's got too much time on his hands. And you're not *latinoamericano*, which makes you fair game."

Laurie swung her gaze back to the man—Gabe?—and started to tell him what she thought of Jimmy's *game*, but instead found herself captivated by his incredible eyes. Dark as bottomless pools on a moonless night, they tangled her normally rational thought processes into spaghetti knots.

Parts of her body which had laid dormant for years tingled to life. Parts of her body which had never been anything *but* dormant tingled to life.

Once again she tried to speak, but Adam was too quick for her. "Wow, that was great! Just like Virgil coming to Dante's rescue in the city of Dis."

Gabe glanced from Laurie to her son, as if trying to decide how to ask discreetly if the boy had lost his mind. "City of—?"

"Comic books!" Laurie said quickly, hoping to God that her brawny savior had never read *The Divine Comedy*. "You know. The Ninja Turtles—Michelangelo, Dante, Virgil."

"Oh, sure," the man said, his expression clearing.

"My nephews are nuts about them. But your son's a lot younger than they are. He must be pretty smart."

"I'm brilliant," Adam announced with unabashed pride.

Laurie cringed. When she got home she would have to have another talk with Adam about keeping his intelligence under wraps, but right now she had to keep this man's suspicions to a minimum. She'd seen the glint of interest in his eyes, and sensed the sharp shrewdness behind his coolly handsome facade. The man was too quick by half. "My son loves comic books, though he mostly looks at the pictures. He's just compared you to his number one hero. It's his way of saying thank you."

He watched her a moment, studying her face with a disconcerting thoroughness. *Now I know how all those lab specimens felt*, she thought bleakly. For a long moment she held her breath, wondering if she'd managed to blow her cover in less than a week. They'd have to move again, to another state, another city, another name . . .

Then Gabe's lips curled into a brief but incandescent smile. "I've never been compared to a comic book hero before."

For a split second Laurie entirely lost the power of speech. Gabe's sensual smile hit her with the searing force of the Mediterranean sun, melting her carefully nurtured doubts and cautions into a useless puddle of wax. Almost thirty years spent as the proverbial ugly duckling hadn't taught her how to deal with a man like him. She stared into the heart of his dark eyes, wondering if he put the passion of his smile into everything he did—laughing, eating, loving . . .

It took every ounce of discipline she'd learned from years of scientific research to pull herself away from the dangerous brink. "I'd like to thank you, as well," she said with a calm she did not feel. "It was lucky for us you were nearby."

Luck had nothing to do with it, Gabe thought grimly. He had been staking out the apartment building for almost an hour, waiting for this woman as a cat waits for a mouse. He'd disguised his intent by talking to his many friends—including the landlord of her building—asking questions too subtle for anyone without a honed investigative mind to follow.

He told himself it was because she was new to his Little Havana neighborhood and he made a practice of checking out recent arrivals. He assured himself it had nothing to do with Yoli's prophecy.

He almost believed it.

"I work in the office across the street, Ms. Palmer," he said, giving her his most calculatingly winning smile. Usually his disarming grin melted a woman's defenses like a blowtorch through butter. Oddly, it seemed to have a completely opposite effect on this lady.

She took a half step back and placed herself between Gabe and her son in an unconscious, but nonetheless unmistakable, stance of defense. "How do you know my name?"

I know a hell of a lot more about you than that, puchunguita. He knew she'd paid her apartment's rent in cash, and that she'd moved in with only a couple of small suitcases of belongings. He'd learned she'd asked around for nearby job openings, and that the only identification she'd shown was a faded out-of-state driver's license. He'd learned that she played classical music in the evenings, and that she and her son had not had a single visitor or made a phone call since their arrival.

She seemed, for all practical purposes, to be entirely alone in the world.

That last point brought Gabe an unaccustomed twinge of guilt. His parents had been killed in a car accident when he was ten and, though he'd been raised by his doting relatives, he'd never forgotten that numbing, helpless feeling of loss and isolation. His calculated smile softened into a more genuine expression. "Yoli told me your name."

"Yoli?" she said, turning puzzled eyes to meet his.

Her eyes. They were as blue as the sea at sunset, a deep indigo that washed against his turbulent soul like a gentle, incessant wave. He stared into them, fascinated by the rare beauty of their color, and the almost childlike intensity of her curiosity.

Gabe lived in a world of intrigue and suspicion, where everyone had a hidden motive and lying was the status quo. Experience had taught him how to deal with everything, from unfaithful husbands, to obsequious embezzlers, and even a thin-lipped drug lord who gave him a piece of lead in his shoulder as a souvenir. Experience had taught him how to deal with everything.

Everything, that is, except innocence.

Suddenly the delicate furrow between her brows cleared. "Yoli, of course," she said, remembering. "You must mean the woman I met at the Laundromat last night. The gypsy queen."

Not again, Gabe thought, groaning inwardly. He'd hoped Yoli had given up introducing herself by one of her past life personas. "The *gypsy queen* is also my secretary," he admitted reluctantly. "She mentioned meeting you."

"That's funny. We didn't talk much. I'm surprised she even remembered me."

As if anyone could forget you. His eyes flickered over her slight, fragile-looking body, birdlike in its delicacy. She reminded him of a little golden parakeet who'd somehow escaped the protection of her cage. It was only a matter of time before some hungry wolf came along and gobbled her up.

He looked into her innocent eyes, and unaccountably found his temper rising. A woman alone should know better than to trust a stranger, he thought with a sudden twist of anger. A woman alone should know better than to trust *him*.

He bent down and swiped up the remaining grocery bag. "You should be more careful about who you trust with your groceries."

She stiffened at the undisguised condemnation in his voice. "I can take care of myself."

He gave a short, unpleasant laugh. "Laurie Palmer, you don't know the first thing about taking care of yourself. Jimmy is harmless, but there are plenty of others who aren't. Little Havana is a tough neighborhood in a tough city. My advice is to pack up your stuff and move back to the suburbs."

"I didn't ask for your advice," she stated with surprising vehemence. "And I can carry my own groceries, thank you."

The corner of his mouth twitched up in amusement. So the little bird had a temper! "*Puchunguita*, the women on my street do not carry groceries."

"This one does."

She made a grab for the bag. Gabe saw the move coming and easily sidestepped it. However, the sudden lunge threw her off balance, causing her to slip on the worn stone steps and pitch forward into space. Cursing, Gabe dropped the groceries and caught her around the waist, narrowly saving her from landing facefirst on the concrete sidewalk. But the force of the rescue sent him off balance as well, and he ended up sitting back hard on the stone steps, holding her astride his lap.

She didn't feel like a bird. Her body was slim and compact, but it was round in all the right places. The soft swell of her breast pressed against his forearm, its gentle pressure sending a raw electric current shooting through his body. It had been a long time since he'd reacted so strongly to a woman. *Dios mío*, she was a pleasure to hold!

The sound of staccato clapping caught his attention. Looking up, he saw Manolo Perez, the apartment building manager, leaning out a second-story window. Sunlight glinted off his smooth, bald head, which shook as he laughed. Then he called out something to Gabe in Spanish—something very funny but very vulgar.

Laurie twisted back to face him. "What did he say?"

Gabe doubted she'd appreciate the unedited version. "He said, uhm, that you don't have much luck with groceries."

"Like hell he did," she commented, a rare smile touching her lips.

Gabe had watched women smile before. He'd held women with far more enticing curves than Laurie's in far more provocative positions. But, until he saw Laurie's hesitant smile and felt the birdlike flutter of her heart beating so close to his own, he hadn't realized how much he'd been missing. The gold in her hair also sparkled in the depths of her indigo eyes, like sunken chests of buried treasure. Deep within him the savage appetites of his buccaneer ancestors stirred to life.

Once a pirate, always a pirate . . .

"Mom, are you okay?" Adam cried, rushing to their aid from the top of the stairs.

"I'm fine," she said, a little breathlessly. "But it seems I owe Mr. Ninja Turtle here another thank-you."

"The name is Ramirez," Gabe answered, equally breathless. Reluctantly he relinquished his hold on Laurie and helped her to her feet. He thought he sensed a reluctance in her as well, and was shocked at how much he wanted her to feel that way.

He didn't need this. He had better things to do with his time than play nursemaid to a pigeon who was ripe for plucking. If she wanted to stay in Little Havana that was her problem, not his. She was trouble with a capital T, and the last thing he needed in his life was more trouble. He backed away down the steps, preparing to leave.

She didn't notice his impending departure because she wasn't looking at him. She stood with her hands on her hips, surveying the double tragedy of her groceries.

"I think Mr. Perez was right. I don't have much luck with groceries. Cooking is definitely out," she said, turning to her son with a sigh. "I'll have to order a pizza for you and the sitter before I leave for work tonight."

"Tonight?" Gabe said, stopping his calculated retreat. The streets were dangerous enough in the daytime, but at night they turned into a war zone. "You shouldn't leave your apartment at night."

Once again she stiffened. "I'm working just a few blocks over, at a place called Shanghai Bill's. Besides, I can—"

"You can take care of yourself," Gabe finished curtly. Bill's, for crissake! There were worse places in the neighborhood, but not many. "Bill's is not the sort of place a woman like you should be working in."

Adam's eyes grew round with interest. "Why not?"

"Never mind," she told her son. She lifted her chin, facing Gabe with more pride than sense. "Besides, Mr. Ramirez doesn't know a thing about me or the kind of places where I've worked."

"Maybe not," Gabe agreed, "but I'm pretty good at making assumptions. You have to be, in my line of work. I'm a private investigator."

Her chin abruptly lost its defiant tilt. She backed away up the steps, her body curling in on itself like a butterfly returning to its cocoon. "Get into the building, Adam," she said quietly.

"But—"

"Now!" she stated, keeping a wary watch on Gabe. "I thank you for your help, Mr. Ramirez, but in the future I'd prefer it if you'd keep away from me and my son."

Gabe's eyes narrowed as he studied her expression, baffled by the sudden change in her. A moment before her cheeks had been flushed with pride and anger. Now her skin was ashen, pale with an almost paralyzing fear. He didn't know the reason for her distress, but he knew that he'd caused it. Instinctively, he reached out to comfort her, but she was too quick for him. With the speed of a bird taking flight she darted up the steps after her son, disappearing into the dark entrance of the building. Gabe's hand closed on empty air.

Who are you running from, corazón?

The memory drifted back to him, the picture of a lovely, golden-haired woman shivering with fear in his arms. Years had passed, but he could still remember how she'd clung to him, pouring out her tears and secrets, making him love her more with each tortured word. Only later, much later, did he learn that every word she'd spoken that night was a lie.

And now he was drawn to another wounded sparrow, equally innocent, equally in need of his protection. Laurie Palmer's eyes were just as guileless as Diana's, and her hair just as golden. But was the ore inside her the twenty-four-karat variety, or just fool's gold?

TWO

Laurie stood in front of the mirror in the ladies' room of Shanghai Bill's and tugged frantically on the hem of her formfitting yellow silk waitress outfit. "It's too short."

One sink over, a perky brunette dressed in an equally abbreviated blue outfit, merely shrugged. "I don't see why you're complaining," she said as she applied a liberal helping of lavender mascara to her lashes. "You definitely have the bod for it. If you've got it, flaunt it, I always say."

"But Gina, what if the customers don't think I've got, er, *it?*"

The brunette interrupted her preening to give Laurie a brief, incredulous look. "Trust me, honey, you've got *it* in spades. Just flash the guys a little leg and a little sass, and you'll have more tips than you know what to do with. Don't worry."

Don't worry, Laurie thought as she stopped tugging her uniform. Worry had been her constant companion for years—she wouldn't know how to live without it. Still, she had to give it a try. She straightened and gave her image a thorough, and what she hoped was an unbiased, appraisal.

Objectively, she decided that she didn't look *too* ridiculous. On Gina's advice she'd swept her hair to the side, allowing the red-gold mass to drape over the front of her shoulder—she was surprised at how long it had grown during the last several months of constant travel. She looked almost . . . sexy.

She took a moment to study her figure as well. The yellow silk clung to curves that were a great deal less generous than they had been a few years before, and her legs, although too exposed for her comfort, were muscular and well defined. She'd noticed the change in her figure before, of course, but she'd never seen the evidence presented quite so—blatantly. Six years of living on the run had turned her pudgy form into a body that a model might have envied. *The fugitive's weight-loss diet*, she thought with a self-deprecating smile. *I should patent it and make a mint.*

A short, concise expletive brought Laurie out of her silent perusal. "Cripes, look at the time!" Gina exclaimed as she stuffed her mascara back into her handbag. "If we're not out in a minute, the boss will fire us for sure."

Working at Shanghai Bill's wasn't Laurie's idea of a dream job, especially since it meant leaving Adam with a sitter for the night. Still, it was the only position she'd been able to find since she'd arrived in

Miami—at least, the only one where the owner hadn't been too picky about a past work history. With her supply of cash getting dangerously low, she needed the job more than she cared to admit. She grabbed up her purse and started to follow Gina out of the bathroom.

Laurie turned too quickly and slipped on a wet tile, coming down hard on her knee. Damn, it smarted. She sucked in her breath and brought her hands to her knee, vigorously rubbing the sore area. Her open handbag dropped to the ground, the contents spilling out on the slick floor. *Not again* . . .

"Are you all right?" Gina asked, kneeling beside her.

"I'm fine," Laurie answered, a little breathlessly. Memories of another savior came to mind, of a melting smile, large, unexpectedly gentle hands, and a pair of gorgeous, too shrewd eyes. Oh hell! She'd spent the better part of the afternoon trying to get Gabe Ramirez's image out of her mind—

A sharp knock on the bathroom door interrupted her thoughts. "Girls, stop primping and get out here!"

"Oh, get a life, man. We'll be out in a second," Gina called back as she scooped up Laurie's spilled belongings and stuffed them back into her purse. "You *are* going to be okay, aren't you?"

Laurie nodded and grasped the sink, using its support to pull herself into a standing position. Her knee ached like crazy, but she could handle it. Living with the minor pains of life had become standard procedure for her. Doctors asked too many questions. She glanced over at Gina, who was just dropping the last of the scattered items, Laurie's dog-eared driver's license, into the purse. With her blue dress and wild lavender makeup the flamboyant brunette looked like a badly wrapped Christmas package, but Gina'd been uncommonly decent to her. Hard experience had taught Laurie that strangers were rarely so kind. "Thank you," Laurie said sincerely. "Not everyone would have stuck around to help."

"Forget it," Gina said as she handed back the purse. "Besides, if I go out there alone, I'd probably have to wait on your tables as well as mine. And honey, my dogs just couldn't take it."

With a final adjustment to their skirts they stepped out into the noisy, crowded atmosphere of Shanghai Bill's. Laurie had worked in dozens of bars over the years, but she'd never seen one quite like this. The plaster walls, painted Miami pink, were covered with a chaotic variety of travel posters and neon signs, with an occasional smattering of pictures of scantily dressed women. Loud, high-tech music vibrated off the walls, adding to the slick, but strangely adolescent mood of the place. The decorator had apparently tried to create an atmosphere of sophisticated decadence, but ended up with something that looked and sounded more like a high school boys' locker room.

It wasn't exactly a den of iniquity, but it was hardly family dining, either. Most of the customers were out-of-state businessmen from small midwestern towns, who mistakenly thought they were indulging in a slice of tropical Miami sin. They wanted to kick their heels up—but not too high—and the pretty waitresses in their skimpy, exotic outfits filled that bill to a tee.

"Skin and sass," Laurie murmured as she strove to follow Gina's advice. She did her best, trying to swing her hips in a provocative manner, and parry the customers' innuendos with sparkling replies. But she soon realized she wasn't any good at it. In her clinging outfit she may have looked the part of a sassy seductress, but inside she was still the same awkward wallflower that she'd always been. She was as bogus as the theme-park decadence of the place, and her customers knew it. Most of them laughed off her nervous clumsiness, but a few took the opportunity to be needlessly cruel.

"Jerk," she muttered as she turned away from a fleshy good old boy who'd complained three times about his drink—loudly. This last time she'd given it back to him unaltered, and he'd proclaimed that it was finally acceptable. Major jerk. For two cents she would have thrown the bourbon and branch water right in his face, but unfortunately she couldn't spare even that much change. She needed the money too much. Lately she'd had to dip into the "getaway" fund, the financial cushion she kept in case she and Adam had to make tracks in a hurry.

She looked out over the noisy, crowded room, watching the kaleidoscope of people—thinking how their voices all sounded familiar and their faces all looked the same. For six years she'd lived in a gray landscape of strangers, never daring to get close to anyone, or to let anyone get close to her. She leaned against one of the room's metallic posts, feeling the isolation of her life close around her like a fist. She didn't regret any of the tough decisions she'd made—she'd make them again in a heartbeat—but sometimes she couldn't help wishing for the things ordinary people took for granted. An apartment she could live in long enough to order address labels. A friend she could talk to without guarding every word. A pair of strong arms to hold her in the night, protecting her from dark dreams, whispering endearments in her ear. . . .

Lord, what was she thinking! She straightened up from the post, embarrassed and shaking from the sexual vividness of the short but potent fantasy. She couldn't face her surly customers in this state, not until she got Gabe's erotic image out of her system. She scanned the room for Gina, intending to ask the brunette to watch her tables for a minute while she stepped outside.

After several passes, she spotted Gina on the far side of the room, talking to a shadowed figure at a dim corner table. *Finally*, she thought as she worked her way through the tightly packed crowd. Gina had helped her out before. Gina, more than anyone she'd met so far, was a real friend.

At least, that's what Laurie thought, until she saw the profile of the man Gina was talking to.

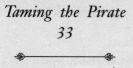

"She's about as dangerous as a newborn lamb," the lanky brunette reported. "Why'd you want me to check up on her?"

Gabe was wondering that himself. If he had a brain he'd be enjoying an intimate dinner at Rachel's, or taking Suzanne out on *Dulcinea* for a midnight cruise under the stars. Instead he was stuck at a back table of this lousy tourist trap, following a woman who wanted his help about as much as she wanted a root canal. Rocks had more sense. "She's new in the neighborhood. Just moved in across the street."

"Oh, like no one's done that before," Gina said archly.

Gabe lifted his scotch to his lips and took a sip, trying his best to ignore Gina Trinadad's comment. She was one of the sharpest detectives in the Miami Police Department, which was why she'd been selected to work undercover at Shanghai Bill's to investigate a possible drug connection. During the years they'd worked together on the force, Gabe had always admired her intelligence, but there were times when he wished she were a little less insightful. Like now. "Lamb's not on my menu," he stated. "She's a mystery, and I don't like mysteries on my street. For example—what's a classy lady like her doing working in a dive like this?"

"I gather it's the only job she could find. I know she's still looking for a daytime job because she doesn't like leaving her son with a sitter at night." She smiled genuinely at the memory. "Lord, she's crazy about that kid of hers."

Gina was right about that, Gabe thought. He remembered the closeness between Laurie and Adam, the looks and gestures that spoke of a deep, caring bond between mother and son. Still, he'd once helped prosecute a bank embezzler who volunteered weekends at orphanages and animal shelters. Kindness and caring didn't necessarily equate to honesty. "Anything else?"

"No. Well, maybe . . ." She drummed her fuchsia-painted fingernails against her chin, looking thoughtful. "It's just a hunch, but you might check out her driver's license. I got a quick look at it. Seemed a little flimsy. It could be a fake."

"Did you get the number?"

Gina shook her head. "Not enough time. But even if her license is a forgery, I still think she's harmless. I like the kid. She's probably just a lamb with a bad driving record."

"Maybe," he said, taking another sip. *Hopefully.* "Thanks for helping me out."

"No problem. Besides, this is one of the cushiest assignments I've ever had. The manager lets me keep whatever tips I make. Sure pays better than being a cop," she said, grinning. "You were smart to get out when you did."

Gabe set his glass carefully on the table. He and Gina both knew why he'd left the force, and *smart* had nothing to do with it. Gina was one of the handful of officers who believed he wasn't party to Diana's crimes. Their superiors, the ones who had demanded his resignation, had not. Later, when an exhaustive investigation had proved his innocence, those same officials had offered him his old job back, with a salary increase if he'd forget the incident ever happened. Gabe had taken great pleasure in telling them exactly what they could do with their hush money. "You're a pal, lady," he said, meaning it. "Thanks again."

"My pleasure, Pirate," she said, using his old nickname from the force. "Wish I could have helped you out more with your mysterious Laurie Palmer." She scribbled something on her pad and handed the sheet to Gabe.

He looked at the short series of digits on the paper. "I thought you said you didn't get her number."

"That's not her number. It's mine," she said, giving Gabe a quick wink. "Catch you later."

Gina, Gabe thought as he watched his friend disappear into the crowd, was always a surprise. During his years on the force dozens of men had lusted after her, himself included, but she rarely gave out her personal phone number. Now he held the sought-after number right in the palm of his hand. She was exactly the kind of woman he wanted in his life—a fun-loving companion who was interested in the present, not the future. By rights he ought to jump at the chance to date her.

He ought to, but he wouldn't.

He turned his dark gaze back to the paper he held in his hand, his smile dissolving into a sobering frown. Looking out for a woman who didn't want his help was one thing, but letting himself fall for her would be just plain stupid. Still, he couldn't deny that she'd stirred him in a way no woman had in a long time.

He'd held her against him for a minute, maybe two, yet he remembered every curve of her slim body, and recalled every beat of her wildly fluttering heart. He also recalled the arctic chill in her eyes when she'd told him to stay away from her. Scowling, he picked up his glass, and downed the remainder in a single toss. Dios mío, if her icy eyes heated his blood, what would happen if she ever looked at him with fire . . . ?

"Mr. Ramirez!"

Gabe winced. The words came from behind his shoulder so he couldn't see the speaker, but there was no mistaking that voice. Husky. Feminine. And mad as hell. Well, that's what he got for coming to the bar in person, instead of waiting at home for Gina's report. Sighing, he set down his glass and turned to face her. "Ms. Palmer, what a pleasant sur—"

He froze, startled to silence by the wealth of gold that met his eyes. She was gleaming fire, from the top of her red-gold head to the glittering yellow sandals on her feet. Her silk dress wrapped her like a golden web, defining sweetly ripe breasts and a waist that looked small enough to span with his hands. Against the backdrop of the low-lighted bar she gleamed like sunken treasure in a murky sea, and his mouth went dry with an ancient, claiming lust.

She shifted uneasily under his gaze. "You don't

have to stare," she said, her voice throaty with embarrassment. "I know I look stupid."

Stupid? She was a golden goddess, the treasures of his ancestors come to life. She was El Dorado, the riches of Montezuma, and Blackbeard's plundered fortune all rolled into one. She was the heart's desire of four hundred years of buccaneer adventurers. He opened his mouth to tell her so, but all he found breath for was, "You look fine."

She crossed her arms defensively, clearly not believing him. The subtle gesture spoke of a lifetime of insecurity, and it twisted through his heart like a tiny knife. *Who are you running from, corazón?*

"This isn't Gina's station. Why was she talking to you?"

He could have lied to her, told her that Gina had simply come over to flirt with him. Knowing Gina's personality he suspected Laurie would believe him. Besides, years as an undercover cop and a private investigator had made him an expert at deception. But as he studied the tilt of her chin, and saw the haunting sadness in her indigo eyes, he knew that he could never willingly lie to her. Someone in her past had hurt this woman—badly. The cryptic description Yoli had used earlier in his office came back to him, suddenly making a strange kind of sense. *The Queen of Swords.*

He raked his hand through his hair and gave her most of the truth. "I asked Gina to help me. I wanted her to keep an eye out for you."

He'd expected his explanation to put her at ease.

Instead, she stiffened, growing more tense than ever. "You sent Gina to spy on me," she said dully. She looked at the ground, her disappointment almost palpable. "I should have known she was helping me for a reason."

"She did want to help you. So do I."

Her head snapped up. Their gazes locked, her eyes meeting his with a canniness he'd rarely encountered in another. This woman was nobody's fool.

Underneath the Bo-peep exterior blazed a shrewd intellect. He appreciated brains, particularly when they were encased in a body as rare and beautiful as the gleaming edge of a golden dagger. But there was something else too—a hint of sadness, a haunting sorrow that dulled the radiant glory in her eyes. He sensed that she'd had more than her share of hardships in her life, and that she'd faced them alone. Someone, somewhere had taught her not to trust. Too late, he realized he'd just reinforced that lesson.

"My son and I aren't charity cases, Mr. Ramirez," she said with stiff, almost melodramatic pride. "We don't need your help."

"Don't be a fool," he answered impatiently. "Reading people is my job, and I know you're in some sort of trouble." His voice softened as he added, "It's no crime to ask for help."

She didn't share his opinion. "I don't need your help," she repeated with a stark finality. "I want you to leave me alone." Then she spun around and faded into the milling crowd.

Gabe had half a mind to go after her, but he

doubted it would do any good. After using Gina to tail her, he doubted Laurie would ever confide in him. But she was in trouble—he knew that like he knew his own name.

"Dammit," he murmured softly, "what *are* you running from?"

If I survive this evening, Laurie thought as she rubbed her pounding temples, *it'll be a miracle worthy of Moses.* Since her confrontation with Gabe her patience had gone from slight to nil, though she'd managed to hide it behind a well-practiced facade of calm. Nevertheless, her temper was rising, increasing along with the volume of the music and the number of people cramming into the already-packed room. She felt like a pressure cooker about to explode.

She picked up a drink order at the bar—major jerk's fourth round—and headed back to her customers. On the way she glanced over at the corner table where Gabe had been sitting, and noted it was occupied by a pair of men in checkered sport coats and ill-fitting toupees. Apparently the private investigator had decided to respect her wishes and leave her alone. The unexpected stab of regret she felt at the knowledge only added to her growing tension.

"Waitress!"

Laurie looked around and saw major jerk standing by his table, glaring at her with small, slightly glassy eyes. Dammit, the man was three-quarters drunk, and his companions weren't in much better shape. She glanced at the collection of drinks on her tray, her integrity overriding her disgust. She turned away, intending to return with a pot of strong coffee, at her expense, if necessary.

Three steps later she felt a hard, clammy hand catch her elbow. "Hey, those are our drinks!"

Laurie sighed wearily, and turned around to face her irate customer. "Don't you think you've had enough?"

He laughed, a short, ugly sound. "Even if I had, I wouldn't let myself be cut off by some *—*."

Laurie cringed at the foul term. She'd been called that name only once before in her life, by the angels —the security guards employed by TechniKon Industries. The white lab coats they wore had earned them their unusual nickname. It became a sort of sick joke among her coworkers—considering the angels had more in common with storm troopers than heavenly beings.

Back then, in order to protect Adam, she'd had to bear their insults in bitter silence. Now she had no such restraints. Without batting an eye she dumped the entire tray of drinks down major jerk's polyester shirtfront. "You want your drinks? You got 'em."

"Why you—" he sputtered. Then his eyes narrowed to weasel slits and his hand shot out, grasping her forearm with a force that made her wince. Memories flooded back, of the windowless basement room, the relentless verbal abuse, the fear. She shuddered, feeling the edge of terror that usually only came to her in her dreams.

"Let her go."

Laurie's whole body went still. Hardly breathing, she watched as Gabe's tiger-lean form materialized out of the crowd and walked slowly to her side. He fastened his dark gaze on her assailant, staring him down with barely concealed menace. "Amigo, I suggest you take my advice."

Major jerk swallowed, releasing Laurie's arm as if it burned him. "But . . . she ruined my suit."

Gabe's look changed from menace to contempt. He pulled a wallet out of his back pocket and thrust several bills into the man's empty hand. "Buy yourself a new one. Now go back to your table before I decide to teach you some manners."

Gabe didn't have to ask twice. The jerk, now stone sober from the shock, scurried away through the crowd like a rat through the underbrush. Gabe watched him until he was safely settled at his table, then he swung his gaze back to Laurie. "Are you all right?"

Laurie shuddered, wondering whether she trembled from her remembered terror or the dark intensity of Gabe's eyes. Piercing and hypnotic, they seemed to bore into her while remaining unreadable themselves. She wrapped her arms around herself, as if she could physically conceal her secrets from his probing gaze. "I'm fine," she said, too brightly. "Thanks for stepping in."

His sensuous lips pulled up in the ghost of a grin. "It seems you needed my help after all."

The man gave new meaning to the word arrogant,

Laurie thought, meeting his eyes with a challenging gaze. Still, she admitted he had reason to be. The people in the bar, like the people on the street this afternoon, automatically drew back to give him space. Friends and strangers alike instinctively accorded him a measure of respect. Laurie, too, felt the undeniable power of his presence, yet she sensed something else as well. As she looked into his midnight eyes she caught a glimpse of a darker shadow, a pain buried so deep that it was almost invisible. She wondered how many people got close enough to see—

"What's happened here?"

The manager's bark brought Laurie back to the present. Lord, she'd hoped this mess would be cleaned up before he found out. She glanced at the pile of broken glass and liquor near her feet, praying the incident didn't cost her, her job. "There was an accident," she began.

The manager's eyes narrowed. "What kind of accident?"

Laurie swallowed. She didn't like to lie, but she didn't have much choice. She needed this job, and if the manager found out what she'd really done, he'd fire her on the spot. "I was carrying drinks to a table and the tray slipped—"

"She dumped a load of drinks on one of your customers," Gabe finished. "On purpose."

The manager gave Laurie a look that said "you're fired" as loud as any words, then moved off through the crowd. Laurie stood for a moment in stunned silence, then turned to Gabe. "Thanks a lot!" she said sarcastically, her voice shaking with the blow of his betrayal.

"I wasn't going to let you continue to work here anyway," he said, apparently not the least perturbed by her show of emotion. He started to leave, motioning her to follow. "Come on. We're getting out of here."

Laurie stared at him, her eyes wide with shock. Arrogance was one thing, but this man was unbelievable. "I have no intention of going anywhere with you."

Gabe stopped. Slowly, he turned around and walked back to her, his steps as precise and deliberate as a tiger stalking its prey. She knew it was only her imagination, but she felt each step physically, crushing the air from her lungs.

His gaze riveted to hers while he spoke, his voice as smooth and lethal as a strangler's silk handkerchief. "I suggest you change your mind, *puchunguita*. Because if you don't walk out of here with me right now, I'm going to throw you over my shoulder like a sack of flour and carry you out."

THREE

Stepping out of the noisy, congested atmosphere of Shanghai Bill's was like entering another world. The sky above was velvet black, its darkness broken only occasionally by the lackluster radiance of an outdated streetlight. Due to the late hour most of the God-fearing residents of Calle Ocho were safely locked behind their front doors, giving the wide, deserted streets an eerie, surreal quality. After sunset the temperature had dropped like a stone in a well, but the cement sidewalks still radiated the heat that had been baked into them by the midday sun. Energy shimmered in the dim, too quiet air, filling Laurie with a strange anticipation. She felt like a stick of dynamite about to be lit. Or a lover about to be kissed.

She wished he would say something.

She stole a glance at the man who walked beside her, his dark presence blending too perfectly with the shadows of the night. Since leaving the bar he hadn't

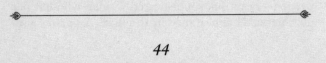

spoken one word or glanced her way, and he kept his hands firmly stuffed in his pockets. She bit her lower lip, feeling an unfamiliar and totally ridiculous ache near her heart. *Would it be so terrible for him if he accidentally touched me?*

"I'll pay you back," she said, unable to stand the silence any longer.

He didn't answer.

"I mean it," she continued, more forcefully this time. "I'll pay back every dollar you gave to that guy. I know you have money to burn, but I don't care. I'm going to pay you back."

Gabe's chuckle surprised her. "Money to burn," he murmured, shaking his head. "That's a laugh." He sighed, hunching his shoulders as he pushed his hands more deeply into his pockets. "I haven't had the kind of money you're talking about for years."

"Then why did you help me?" she asked, perplexed. "You had no reason to. Unless . . . well, you weren't expecting me to . . . I mean, you didn't think I would—"

He glanced at her, lifting an eyebrow in wry amusement. "I have no need to pay for *that*, *puchunguita*."

Laurie felt her cheeks burn, glad that the cover of night hid her embarrassment. Talk about stupid! On a ten-point "gorgeous" scale, Gabe Ramirez registered a solid eleven. With his incredible looks and smooth Latin charm he probably had his pick of a dozen women—beautiful, sophisticated women who left her unremarkable appearance in the dust. A person with her IQ should have been able to figure that out without making a total fool of herself. She wrapped her arms around herself, feeling every inch the awkward, ugly duckling she'd been in her past.

Suddenly she felt the gentle brush of fingers against her arm. "Are you sure you're all right?"

All right? His light touch sent every nerve in her body into overdrive. Her mind flashed back to earlier that day, when she'd accidentally tumbled into his arms. Their brief embrace had been Disney-pure, hardly the stuff fantasies are made of, yet just the memory made her short of breath. She'd felt the hard wall of his chest against her back, the coiled strength of his arms as he'd rescued her from falling. She'd felt the intensity within him, the seething energy sizzling beneath his outwardly calm exterior.

For a moment she'd drawn on that energy, letting his power replenish her own weary senses, resting in the comforting protection of his arms. For a moment. Then she'd remembered that her savior was a complete stranger, a man who knew nothing about her, not even her real name. If he knew the truth, he'd most likely dump her back on the concrete and run for the hills. Or betray her, as so many others she'd trusted had done. . . .

She quickened her step, purposely putting herself out of his reach. "How do you expect me to feel?" she said, counterfeiting a shrewishness that was not in her nature. "You just helped get me fired. Am I supposed to thank you for that?"

"A woman like you doesn't belong in a place like that."

He spoke with the certainty of Moses handing down the commandments. Damn him for caring, she thought angrily. And double damn him for being right. "A woman like me," she said bluntly, "doesn't have a whole lot of choices. I need a job, Mr. Ramirez. I've got a son to support."

"Don't you get alimony, or child support?"

"I've never been married," she answered without thinking, then winced as she realized what that implied. Loose morals, easy virtue. Lord, what he must think of her! "I mean, it was so long ago that I *feel* like I've never been married," she amended. "Adam's father . . . died."

"Forgive me," he stated quietly. "I did not mean to add to your grief."

He sounded so genuinely sincere that she felt guilty. Hell, now he thought she was a grieving widow. "Well, like I said, it happened a long time ago," she said, trying to make up for lying to him. "Anyway, I still need a job."

"Okay, what are you qualified to do?"

She grinned slightly, wondering what he would say if she told him the truth. Biological researcher and genetic engineer weren't exactly the most common occupations—Lord, wouldn't a private investigator have a field day with those professions!

"I've done just about everything," she told him. It was an honest answer. During the past six years, she had.

He rubbed his chin, deep in silent thought. For a moment his attention was elsewhere, and she took the opportunity to openly study him.

He was an incredibly beautiful man. Yet, it wasn't only his surface looks which attracted her. There was an inner strength about him, an intensity that drew her like a magnet to steel. He had the natural charisma of a man who could lead a company of soldiers into an impossible battle, or a band of cutthroat pirates into an attack on a well-armed ship. Men like him lived by their own rules, and they didn't give a damn if the world approved. Right or wrong, he would take a stand and fight for what he believed in. Even if it was an unpopular position. Even if he hadn't a hope in hell of winning.

What if he *could* help her?

"Can you run a cash register?" he asked suddenly.

The very ordinary question brought her soaring hopes thudding back to reality. "Yes, I worked in a convenience store last summer."

"Fine. My aunt owns a grocery store a few blocks over, and she's been looking for someone to work the register. You can start in the morning."

Laurie felt as if the gearshift on her life had just been pushed into overdrive. *Tomorrow morning?* "But I can't. I have to find a day sitter for Adam. And I know your aunt will want some sort of work references."

"Two of my cousins live in apartments over the store. They watch other neighborhood kids during the day—I'm sure they wouldn't mind watching your

son. As for references," he said, flashing her a con-
spiratorial smile, "I'll just tell her how you dumped
that tray of drinks on the guy in the bar. Aunt Berta
loves a woman who won't take guff from a man. I
suppose it comes from living with her brother, my
uncle Carlos. He's a bit of a rascal. . . ."

As they continued their walk home Gabe told her
about his mixed bag of relatives. The night was still
dark and the street still lonely, but Gabe's entertaining stories drove away a little of the gloom. She
learned about his strong-willed aunt Berta, who had
taken over the store when her husband passed away,
and had run it single-handed for twenty years. But
Laurie was especially enchanted by Gabe's tales of his
charming but unscrupulous uncle Carlos, a lawyer by
profession, and a scoundrel by nature.

Laurie had spent her youth being shuttled between boarding schools by her wealthy, self-centered
mother. Deprived of a normal childhood, she'd com-
pensated by burying herself in books, using storybook
characters to fill the emptiness in her heart. Years ago
she'd grown out of her childhood loneliness—or con-
vinced herself that she had—until Gabe reminded her
of what she'd been missing. She absorbed the stories
of his lively, eccentric relatives like a sponge soaks up
water. By the time they reached her apartment door
she was laughing right along with him, more at ease
with Gabe than she'd ever been with another person
in her life.

"You haven't told me yet if you're going to take

the job," Gabe said as he took Laurie's key and opened her door.

"How can I resist?" she said, still smiling. "I've got to see these people for myself. They can't possibly be as crazy as you say they are."

"You doubt my word?" he intoned, clutching his heart in mock drama. "I'm wounded."

Laurie laughed. "I think there's a little Uncle Carlos in you, Mr. Ramirez."

"Gabe," he said, fastening his gaze on hers. "Call me Gabe."

Suddenly everything changed. His dark eyes pierced her with a hypnotic intensity, searching out her secrets like a hawk searching for prey. He absorbed her, stealing her breath and speeding her heart. The narrow apartment hallway forced her to stand close to him, making her overwhelmingly aware of his size, his strength, of the way his thick hair fell rakishly across his brow. But most of all she sensed the raw, barely restrained energy that seethed just beneath his deceptively polished exterior. His charming stories had lulled her into a false sense of security, making her forget what his potent masculinity did to her common sense. And what it did to her body. . . .

"Why are you helping me?" she asked quietly, her voice barely above a whisper.

She'd asked him the same question before, and he hadn't answered. He didn't answer her now—at least not in words. Still, she thought she saw the determined line of his jaw lose some of its harshness, and imagined she caught a hint of softness buried in the depths of his eyes. His gaze delved into hers with an intensity that bordered on physical force, but this time she didn't turn away. It may have been the late hour, or the emotional strain of being hired, fired, and hired again in a single day. But whatever the reason, she wasn't afraid anymore.

He searched her eyes for secrets, but she knew instinctively that the secrets he was looking for weren't the kind that could hurt her or her son. The standards she used to judge other men would never apply to Gabe Ramirez. His nature made him a giant among men, set apart from others by the sheer power of his presence. Many people might envy his kind of uniqueness, but Laurie knew better.

She'd seen what being *different* could do to a person. It led to distance and isolation, and a kind of loneliness that ordinary people couldn't begin to imagine. Wordlessly she lifted her hand and brushed soothing fingers across the side of his cheek, thinking how often she'd done the same for her son. Only Adam's cheeks weren't rough with the faint coarseness of beard stubble. And Adam's eyes didn't burn into hers like twin dark suns. . . .

"Well!" came a nearby voice of condemnation.

Jarred out of her imaginings, Laurie looked past Gabe's shoulder to the frumpy, curler-topped figure of her neighbor Mrs. Prima. The older woman stared at the couple, obviously imagining the worst. *Great, a bad rep with the neighbors. That's all I need.* "Good evening, Mrs. Prima. We were just—"

"I was just walking Mrs. Palmer home, Lucila," Gabe interrupted, turning around.

Mrs. Prima's sour face broke into a radiant smile. "Gabe, I didn't know it was you." She wagged her finger at him in gentle rebuke. "You never come to visit me and Pepe anymore."

Gabe gave an easy laugh. "Forgive me, dear heart. I promise to stop by for a proper visit—if I can curb my envy of that lucky husband of yours."

Mrs. Prima blushed like a schoolgirl at his teasing. There was nothing mean spirited or mocking in Gabe's statement—Laurie could tell there was real affection between the two. Part of Gabe's natural charm was that he was generous with his praise, but never phoney. He was kind to everyone. Delinquent kids like Jimmy, aging coquettes like Lucila Prima, even plain, unremarkable single mothers like herself.

I have no need to pay for that, puchunguita.

Her cheeks grew hot with embarrassment. Dammit, Gabe was only trying to be kind, and she'd foolishly mistaken it for something much more. She'd stroked his cheek, for heaven's sake, and her fingers still burned from the touch. He probably thought she was one of those lonely, desperate females. Lord, for a moment, she had been. . . .

"Thank you for the job offer," she said, turning toward the door. "Please tell your aunt I'll be there in the morning."

"Laurie, is something wrong?"

She didn't dare look at him. He'd see the red stain

on her cheeks, the ridiculous longing in her eyes. God help her, he might even try to be nice about it.

"Thank you for your kindness, Mr. Ramirez," she said, hating her coldness but having no other choice. She opened her apartment door and darted inside. Immediately she was enveloped in the arms of her clever child, who'd managed to talk yet another sitter into letting him stay up late. *Adam, Adam, you don't know how much I needed this hug.*

Outside, Gabe stood in the hallway, staring in confusion at the firmly shut door. Questions spun through his mind, and the thread of a hurt he couldn't put a name to. "It's Gabe," he whispered to the locked door. "Gabe."

She hadn't spotted him yet.

Gabe stood behind the pasta-and-rice shelf in his aunt's grocery story, surreptitiously studying Laurie as she rang up customer purchases on the loud, behemoth cash register. It wasn't the first time he'd hidden behind one of the stacks to watch a pretty girl at the checkout counter, but it was the first time he doubted his sanity for doing it.

Why are you helping me?

She'd asked him that question twice last evening, and both times he'd avoided answering it. Avoided, hell. He didn't *have* an answer. He had a desk piled high with case files. He had a rent payment that was overdue. He had a demonic air conditioner, and a secretary who believed herself to be a reincarnated gypsy queen. In short, he didn't have time to play knight errant to a woman he barely knew, who seemed determined to keep it that way.

And yet here he was, skulking behind the pinto beans like some hormone-crazy teenager, watching a woman with golden hair smile at customers in a way she'd never smiled at him.

Well, not *never*. Just before Lucila Prima's untimely arrival Laurie *had* smiled at him—with her lips, her eyes, and especially her heart. He'd taken one look in those huge, hauntingly innocent eyes of hers, and forgotten all about his piled up case files, Yoli, *El Diablo*. . . . *Dios mío*, he'd forgotten his own name! He'd stared into those indigo depths, bewitched by the simplicity of her trust, the artless way she revealed more of herself to him than any woman had before. Then she'd stroked his cheek, caressing him with a sweetness that made him ache for more. Something soft and sacred had stirred in his heart. Something hard and very unsacred had stirred elsewhere.

And still did.

"She's a pretty package, your golden canary," said a voice near his elbow.

Gabe gave a scowl to the older man at his side. "Shhh, *Tío Carlos*. She'll hear you."

"Ha! with all the racket the register is making? She couldn't hear a Mardi Gras parade over that thing." Carlos cocked his head, looking up at his nephew with a canny smile on his face. "I think you did not tell Berta the whole truth about this little bird."

Gabe stiffened. Of all his shrewd relatives, Carlos was by far the most insightful. And the least trustworthy. Before Castro's takeover Carlos Ramirez had made and spent a fortune at the gambling tables of Havana. After he'd arrived in the States he'd made and spent a couple more. His reputation as a topflight trial lawyer was substantial, but his reputation as a gambler was legendary.

When Gabe's mother and father had died, Carlos had taken the orphaned youngster under his wing, involving him in so many scrapes and adventures, the boy didn't have time to miss his parents. Carlos's love and attention had helped the lonely child work through his grief, and Gabe loved the older man with a fierceness that defied description. But he didn't trust him worth a damn. "Don't you have a horse race to handicap? Or a bingo game to fix?"

"I've given up bingo," Carlos sniffed, straightening the crisp collar of his elegant shirt. "Too many old women. Now the little bird is much more my style."

"Don't bet on it, *Tío*. She won't give you the time of day."

"You speak from experience, I assume," Carlos commented, undaunted. "I suppose I'll have to show you how it's done."

Before Gabe could stop him Carlos stepped out from behind the beans and sauntered over to the counter.

Laurie had just finished ringing up the last of a long line of customers when he arrived. She'd been diligently concentrating on mastering the old register, wanting to do the best possible job for her employer Berta. The large, motherly woman had met Laurie with open arms and insisted she call her *tía*, the Spanish word for aunt. Touched by Berta's generous affection, Laurie had put her heart into the job, battling both the museum-piece register and the language barrier as she checked out what seemed to be an endless stream of shoppers. All shapes and sizes of people had passed her station, but none as remarkable as the little, nattily dressed man who approached her now.

The man had style, an old-world elegance that made her think of European aristocracy and the sunny Riviera. His mane of white hair was as fashionably cut as his silk suit, which looked as if it had been tailored just for him. He walked up to the counter and leaned casually against it, flashing her a devilish grin. "Your hair is the color of sunshine, and your eyes are as blue as the Caribbean sea."

Instead of being shocked, Laurie smiled back. She'd seen that grin before on another man's face, though at that time the expression had turned her bones to water. In any case, it gave away the identity of her delightful stranger. "You must be Uncle Carlos."

"Beauty and brains," Carlos said, shaking his head in mock astonishment. "It is a puzzle."

"What is?" she asked, blushing at the compliment.

Uncle Carlos gazed out at the grocery stacks. "Why my foolish nephew prefers the company of pinto beans to that of a beautiful woman."

Laurie heard the pinto beans give a sharp oath. She watched in surprise as Gabe rounded the corner and stalked toward the register, his expression dark as storm clouds. Quickly her surprise turned to another emotion. Dressed in loose khaki slacks and a white cotton boat shirt, he looked as elegant as his uncle, but in a more potent, viral way. Stud—casual style, Laurie thought as he approached. Damn, does he always have to look like he just stepped out of the pages of GQ?

"I guess you want to know why I was standing over there watching you," he said.

Laurie probably would have, if coherent thought had been possible. His liquid baritone slid across her skin like sweet, molten honey. In the past, she'd delivered scientific papers to crowds of thousands. But in the presence of this one particular man she was as tongue-tied as a first-year grad student. Unable to speak, she nodded her head in vague agreement.

"I was concerned about you. I mean, this job was sort of my idea." He raked his hand through his hair, suddenly looking as young as Adam. "I just wanted to make sure you were doing okay."

"I'm fine," she assured him. "Adam's fine too. Your aunt Berta is very sweet."

"Yeah. Guess she is." Silence.

"She couldn't have been nicer." More silence.

"Oh sweet Jesus!" Uncle Carlos exclaimed. "You two are hopeless. Just ask her out, Gabriel, and get it over with."

"*Tío*—" Gabe said dangerously.

Many a strong man had turned to jelly under Gabe's threatening gaze. Uncle Carlos didn't even blink. "Don't use that tone with me, boy," he said, calmly adjusting his cuffs. "I helped change your diapers. Now, ask the lady out. If you don't," he added, turning his buccaneer grin on Laurie, "then I will."

Gabe tried to hold on to his anger at his incorrigible uncle, but the task proved too much for him. Gradually his stormy expression softened with the hint of a reluctant smile. He glanced over at Laurie, his brow arched in pure devilment. "Seems we don't have much choice, *puchunguita*."

"I guess not," she said, her voice barely above a whisper. His eyes consumed her, pulling her into their depths like dark, swirling whirlpools. There didn't seem to be an ounce of air left in her lungs, and her heart slammed so loud against her ribs, she was amazed he didn't hear it. *Lord, if he could do that with just a look—*

"How much?" an impatient voice interrupted.

Laurie turned sharply, and nearly bumped noses with a fleshy-faced woman who leaned across the counter, holding a bunch of guavas. A line of customers was already starting to form behind her. Oddly enough, Gabe's uncle was nowhere in sight. "Where's Carlos?"

"He's probably gone to cause more trouble," Gabe answered, only half joking. He looked at the growing line of customers, regretting the interruption. Every time he began to get close to this woman, to solve the mysteries buried beneath the surface of those bewitching indigo eyes, someone or something broke them apart. It was beginning to get on his nerves. He started to walk away, reluctantly giving her back to her customers. "Berta doesn't open on Saturday," he called back over his shoulder, "so you'll have tomorrow off. I'll pick you up at ten in the morning."

"Wait," she cried. "I can't go. I can't leave Adam—"

"Bring him too," Gabe replied, glancing back.

The glow of appreciation in her eyes should have warmed his heart. Instead, it set off a warning siren in his mind. She was so innocent. So damnably trusting. *Careful, Gabe, or this little golden bird will fly straight into your heart.*

Just like Diana.

The bitter pain struck him anew, sharp and deadly as a serpent's bite, even after all this time. He turned away quickly, and walked out the main store into the back office, where *Tía Berta* sat on those rare occasions when she had nothing better to do. Now wasn't one of those times. The room was deserted, and Gabe sank down into the old leather chair, feeling as if the weight of the world had suddenly settled around his shoulders.

Diana. He'd loved her with all the passionate fury in his pirate's heart, and that love had cost him dearly. He'd believed her tearful stories about being the victim, the innocent pawn in the drug-smuggling operation he'd been investigating. He continued to believe

in her until the bitter end, when with her dying words
she told him how she'd played him for a fool, and
how much pleasure she'd taken in doing it. . . .

Trusting Diana had cost him his career, his honor,
and almost his life. She'd given him a crash course in
treachery and deceit, showing him that a woman
could love a man with her body while she laughed at
him in her heart. The shame of his foolishness still
twisted inside him, even after all these years. He'd
sworn he'd never let a woman get to him again. He'd
kept that vow—so far.

He shook his head, as if he could physically shake
out the memories of Diana's betrayal. In doing so, his
wandering eye caught sight of a familiar object half
hidden in a far corner of the office. Laurie's purse.

Another time he might have left the purse alone,
respecting Laurie's privacy. But not now. He was set
on convincing himself that she was just another case
to him, just a mystery he pursued as diligently as his
ancestors pursued their golden treasures. He scooped
up the purse and riffled efficiently through the contents, extracting the license which Gina had mentioned the night before. It did seem suspiciously
flimsy. He jotted down the number in his pocket
notebook, also noting the birth year of his mysterious
subject. *Thirty-five. Two years older than I am*, he calculated with a frown. *Dios*, it didn't take a private investigator to know she was years younger than that.

As he returned her driver's license, another item
in the purse commanded his attention. Eyes narrow-
ing with interest, he reached in and pulled out a scrap

of paper, the edge of a torn sheet of company letterhead. It was yellowed and creased, clearly the remains of a note that had long since been ripped up and discarded. The content of the letter probably had been consigned to the garbage long ago, but the name of the company remained, repeated over and over again in a decorative border around the edge. "TechniKon," he read aloud.

Now what was his golden bird doing with a piece of letterhead from one of the nation's biggest defense contractors?

FOUR

Saturday morning dawned bright and clear, yet Laurie's mood was anything but sunny. She looked out her bedroom window at the blue sky dotted with fleecy white clouds, imagining that each one was a wolf in sheep's clothing. Turning away, she gave her hair another punishing brush. "I had no choice," she muttered. "It would have looked suspicious if I'd turned him down. It's not like I want to go out with him or anything."

A small, nagging voice in the back of her mind said otherwise.

Laurie winced, wishing her conscience wasn't so demanding. She dropped her brush on the bed and paced the room, talking out her frustration. "Okay, so maybe I *do* want to go out with him. Is that a crime? Besides, it's a daytime date, nothing serious. What could happen?"

The small, nagging voice told her exactly what could happen. In every temptingly erotic detail. . . .

A honking horn interrupted her thoughts. "He's here!" Adam called from the living room. "Mommy, Gabe's here!"

Lord, he's early! she thought as she looked down at the nightshirt she still wore. Fighting panic she stepped over to her bureau and pulled out a blue T-shirt and white shorts, grateful for once that her nomadic lifestyle had taught her how to dress in a hurry. In less than a minute she was out the door of her apartment and heading down the stairs, giving a list of last-minute instructions to her son.

"Now remember. No Dante. No Shakespeare. And definitely no calculus."

"I know, I know," Adam replied in a long-suffering voice. "You always say that. Mommy, why is it bad to be smart?"

"It's not bad, darling. It's—"

They'd reached the bottom of the stairs and were standing in the foyer of the building. Laurie stopped and glanced around, making certain that the hallway leading back to the first floor apartments and the stairway above them was completely deserted. Even then, Laurie didn't take any chances. She knelt down beside her son and spoke to him in a voice just above a whisper. "Your intelligence is just one of our special secrets. You know, the ones we don't want anyone else to know about."

"If someone finds out, will the bad men come and take you away from me?"

The youthful anguish in her son's tone cut through Laurie like a knife. She pulled her son to her, hugging him fiercely. "Adam, no one is going to take me away from you. I promise."

"But if the bad men come—"

"Then we'll go somewhere else. We have before."

Adam appeared to consider her words for a moment. Then he drew back, and looked at her with eyes that had seen far too much for a boy of his age. "But what happens," he asked quietly, "when we run out of places?"

"What kind of places?" a deep voice behind them asked.

Laurie's head shot up. Gabe stood in the hallway near the front door, his tall form leaning casually against the doorframe. She'd been so focused on Adam that she hadn't noticed when he'd entered the building. How long had he been standing there in the hallway, watching them?

How much had he heard?

"Gabe!" Adam cried happily, oblivious to the tension between the adults. Without a moment's hesitation he launched himself toward his friend.

While some men would have shied away from the child's overt affection, Gabe accepted it as if it were the most natural thing in the world. He bent down and caught up Adam, holding the boy easily in his arms. Laurie felt her heart give a sudden, tender twist. Few people had taken the trouble to show Adam any kind of attention during their travels. Yet Gabe had gone out of his way for her son—she knew from

Gabe's cousin that he'd even stopped by to say hello to the boy. It was an uncommonly generous thing for the man to do. She just wished she could trust his motives.

Gabe held the door open for her. "You look very beautiful this morning," he said as she passed.

Laurie remembered her hasty dressing, and the fact that she hadn't had enough time to finish brushing her hair or put on makeup. Realistically she suspected that the *last* thing she looked this morning was beautiful. "Thanks, but you don't have to flatter me," she said honestly. "I got a look at myself in the mirror as I left the apartment."

"Then you should have taken another look, *puchunguita*," he said softly.

She looked up and saw his gaze on her, intense and frankly admiring. A delicious terror shivered through her. She knew without a doubt that he'd meant the compliment sincerely, and that he did find her beautiful. The knowledge disturbed her more than anything had in a long time.

Once again Adam broke the tension between them. "You're early, Gabe. Why did you come so early?"

Gabe set the boy on his feet at the top of the outside stairs. He glanced up into the picture-perfect sky, then looked back down at Adam with an easy smile. "Because it's a sin to waste even a moment of a gorgeous day," he said as they started down the steps. "And because we have several stops to make before I introduce you to *Dulcinea*."

The woman's name caught Laurie's attention. "Who's Dulcinea?"

Gabe turned to Laurie, his eyes flashing with a devilish gleam. "That's my secret. And we all have our secrets, don't we . . . ?"

They climbed into Gabe's car, a sports model that was several years old but still in prime condition, and started on their way. Laurie quickly learned that the "several stops" Gabe mentioned meant picking up "several children," three to be exact. Her erstwhile thief Jimmy was among them.

Along the way, Gabe explained to her that he liked to get the children out of the neighborhood to give them a different view of the world. "Some kids spend their whole lives in Little Havana," he told her. "There are whole blocks where nothing but Spanish is spoken. I try to show them there's something else beyond the barrio."

A shout from the backseat suddenly made Laurie anxious for her young son's safety. She turned around —and saw Adam roughhousing with the others, clearly having the time of his life.

She smiled in relief, and leaned back against the comfortable bucket seat. "Well," she said pleasantly, "so far this qualifies as the *largest* date I've ever been on."

Gabe had the grace to look contrite. "I was afraid that if I told you about the boys, you wouldn't want to come."

"Why not?"

He gave her a melting smile. "Not every woman would willingly spend her day with a bunch like this."

Not every man, either, she thought, looking at Gabe in a new light. A lot of people gave lip service to helping underprivileged kids, but few men would have sacrificed their Saturday for them. Yet, she realized Gabe must do this kind of thing on a regular basis, and she admired him for it. *Careful,* an inner voice warned. *Lusting after him is one thing. But now you're beginning to like the guy . . .*

She turned away and stared out the window, noticing vaguely that they were passing by a marina. She didn't really see much of the scenery, however. She was too busy trying to make sense of her confused emotions. "I suppose . . . I suppose Dulcinea is one of these exceptional women."

"She's exceptional, all right," Gabe agreed.

She heard the genuine affection in his voice. Gabe obviously cared a great deal for this Dulcinea, and Laurie winced at the uncharacteristic sting of jealousy. "If she's so wonderful, I'm surprised you wanted me and the kids along."

She expected Gabe to show a little remorse at not telling her about the other woman. Instead, his smile deepened. "You'll understand when you meet her," he said with maddening cheerfulness. "There she is."

Gabe pulled the car into one of the marina parking spaces, and pointed through the windshield at the assembled boats. Dozens of people moved in and around the ships like a collection of industrious ants.

It was impossible to know which woman Gabe was pointing to. "Who?" she asked.

"She's not a who," he said as he got out of the car and started around to her side.

Laurie peered through the windshield at the marina, still not understanding him. Then she saw the long white sloop lying in one of the nearest slips. Between the dock posts and the people passing by she could only make out the first three letters of the name painted in gold on the side. In this case, however, three letters were enough. "Dul," she said aloud, feeling it fit in more ways than one.

"I owe you for that," she said wryly as he opened her car door.

Gabe's smile widened. He started to say something, but stopped. The four boys had already piled out of the car, and were making a beeline for the refreshment stand. "Hey, crew," he called, cupping his hands around his mouth for extra volume, "get on board and prepare to cast off. We've got to leave now or we'll never make the reef by one!"

"We're going out on the ocean?" Laurie asked as she stepped out of the car.

Gabe walked around to the trunk and pulled out a cooler and a duffel bag. "Well, we could sit at the dock all day, but I think sailing might be more fun. Don't tell me you're afraid of the water?"

It wasn't *water* she was afraid of. When she'd agreed to spend the day with Gabe, she'd imagined they'd be at a park or the beach, safely surrounded by a multitude of other people. She'd never anticipated being virtually alone with him on a boat in the middle of the ocean, with only four underage chaperones for company.

It wasn't her virtue she feared for—it was her secrets. Gabe was a master at getting people to open up to him. That was, after all, his profession. While the kids were playing she and Gabe would have only each other for company. She'd look into the dark surety of his eyes and be tempted to trust him, to tell him the secrets that had weighed on her soul for years. *Danger*, her mind whispered. Every ounce of her common sense told her to call a cab for her and Adam and retreat to the safety of her apartment, before she got herself into a situation she was almost sure to regret—

"Mommy, look. I'm a sailor!"

Laurie glanced over and saw Adam wave to her from the bow of Gabe's ship, where Jimmy was diligently fitting him with a life vest. Adam's smile outshone the sun. Laurie looked at her son, thinking how much he'd changed from the silent, frightened boy who'd sat beside her on the night bus to Miami two weeks ago, too scared to close his eyes for fear the "bad men" would catch them. He'd been so exhausted by the time they arrived that she'd had to carry him through the station.

Laurie's heart constricted in her chest. She'd always prayed that Adam could live a normal life just like other little boys. Now he had a chance to have that ordinary kind of life—even if only for an afternoon. She could certainly endure a day alone with

Gabe for her son's sake. Hell, she would endure a day in purgatory for Adam.

And as she watched Gabe carry the heavy cooler to his boat, muscles rippling across his broad back with every easy stride, she suspected that a day in purgatory was *exactly* what she'd just signed herself up for.

He loved the sea. He loved the feel of the salt wind stinging his cheeks, and the shifting blue landscape stretching from horizon to horizon, shimmering with the light of the sun. Cotton clouds slipped their lazy way across the heavens, charitably deciding to hold their rain and thunder for another day, another country. No two days were the same on the water—no two moments. The ocean was always different, always a challenge, like mastering a thirty-foot sloop, or seducing a beautiful woman.

Both thoughts were very much on Gabe's mind as he held *Dulcinea*'s tiller steady on course, and watched Laurie secure the mainsail rope. The wind tumbled her unbound hair around her face, weaving its red-gold glory with sunlight and shadow. She looked as innocent as a child, as free and untamed as the ocean itself. Only if he stepped closer would he catch a glimpse of the worry that haunted her eyes.

Who are you running from, corazón?

He still had no answer. He'd run both her license number and the reference to TechniKon through Yoli's computer, with mixed results. Oh, the license was a forgery but, as Gina had pointed out, a counterfeit license could mean nothing more than a bad driving record. As a precaution he'd run Adam's description through the missing child data base, but had found no match. Laurie's description, bounced against the F.B.I. criminal files, had also yielded nothing.

It was frustrating. After hours of investigation he wasn't any closer to finding out who this beautiful woman was, or what terrible secret stole the light from her bewitching indigo eyes—

"Can I steer?" a muffled voice near his elbow asked.

Gabe glanced down and saw Adam standing at his side, his small form almost completely enveloped by an ungainly life vest. The bright orange padding effectively hid his chin and mouth, but his eyes shone clearly over the edge. He looked at Gabe with a strange mixture of hope and apprehension, as if he'd grown used to wanting things he knew he could never have.

"Sure," Gabe said without a moment's hesitation. He picked up the boy and held him in his lap, patiently showing him the rudiments of guiding a boat. Under Gabe's gentle tutoring Adam learned quickly, his confidence and happiness increasing by the moment.

"Amigo, you are a born sailor," Gabe said, astonished and pleased at how well the boy was doing. "There must be pirate blood in you somewhere."

"I don't think so," Adam answered seriously. "Mommy didn't put any pirate in me."

That's a strange way of phrasing it, Gabe thought. But then, Adam and his mother were a strange pair. They were like icebergs—with only their tops showing and the rest hidden from view. "Well," Gabe continued, "your mommy isn't the only one who could have had pirate blood. Maybe your daddy had some pirate blood in him."

Still concentrating on his steering, Adam shook his head. "I didn't have a daddy."

"Adam!"

Both Gabe and Adam looked up at once. Laurie stood nearby, her face pale as a ghost. She reached over and took her son from Gabe's lap, setting him on the ground. "Run up front and help the other boys."

Once Adam was out of earshot she turned to Gabe with barely contained rage. "How dare you? How could you use a little boy like that?"

"Use your . . . Lady, what are you talking about?"

"I'm talking about pretending to be my son's friend, then pumping him for information. Of all the low, slimy, underhanded things to d—"

She got no further. Gabe's hand shot out and clasped her wrist in a viselike grip, pulling her hard against him. "Understand, *puchunguita*," he whispered in a voice that raised hair on the back of her neck, "if I wanted to know about you, I would not need to ask your son. *You* would tell me."

"Let me go," she said hoarsely.

"Not yet." He pulled her closer until his lips were inches from hers, until he could feel her shallow breath on his cheek. "I am Adam's friend. And yours. If you would trust me just a little, you would see that."

"But you were questioning him . . ."

"And I found out that you haven't given him the speech about the birds and the bees yet." The edge of his mouth crept up in a rakish grin. "Perhaps you could use a refresher course?"

"Oh, you are so . . ."

Gabe's smile broadened. "Good. A reaction. I was afraid there wasn't a real woman in there."

"I'm real," she said, her words so quiet, they were barely a whisper.

She smelled like the sea. He could feel the heat of the sun in her hair and on her skin, burning through his blood like a primal fire. He'd hungered for women before, and knew the storm of passion like he knew his own name. But he had never known a woman whose touch ignited such an ache inside him, whose smell intoxicated him like Cueva Gold, and whose fathomless eyes made him yearn to discover the buried secrets of her body, even if he had to sell his soul to discover them—

"Reef ahoy!"

Jimmy's call broke the moment between them. Gabe released Laurie's wrist and she stepped back, watching him with the wariness of a deer released from a trap. She rubbed her wrist and opened her mouth to say something, but no words came. He saw the question in her eyes, the need to trust him, and the fear of that need.

"Laurie," he whispered, reaching out.

He was too late. A split second before he spoke she sprinted away, heading toward the front of the boat to assist the boys. She'd made her decision on whether to trust him or not.

She'd decided against him.

I ought to have my brain examined, Laurie thought as she sat alone on *Dulcinea*'s rear dock. The others splashed in the water off to her right, diving down through the clear water to the bright, multicolored treasures of North America's last living coral reef. She kicked her legs in the water, feeling its warmth close seductively around her thighs. A different kind of heat pooled in her center. *And maybe not just my brain.*

She'd almost confided in him. If Jimmy's call hadn't interrupted them, she would have ended up in Gabe's arms, willingly trading her secrets for just one kiss from his seductive lips. She shivered, thinking how close she'd come to opening up to him. Worse, she knew how much she wanted to trust him, how much she *still* wanted to—

"Not swimming, *puchunguita?*"

Startled, she looked up. Gabe held the edge of the floating platform, only his head and shoulders visible above the water. Drops slid across his wet-sleek skin and down the corded column of his muscular neck. Laurie swallowed, trying not to think how much he resembled an ancient sea god, newly risen from the depths. "No, I'm not. I . . . well, I never learned how."

Gabe's eyes widened in surprise, as if she'd just admitted she'd never learned how to breathe. He glanced over to where Adam bobbed up and down in his colorful life vest, playing and laughing with the other boys.

"I wanted Adam to learn," she said in answer to Gabe's unspoken question. "I've taken him to several YMCA classes, and I think he'll be a wonderful swimmer."

"Your parents never took you to classes?" Gabe asked.

She studied the water, watching her leg make slow circles in the ocean she'd never been in. "There was only my mother, and she kept me at boarding schools for most of my early years. The only time I ever saw her was holidays, and then only when the schools couldn't arrange other accommodations for me." She glanced up, focusing on the distant, lonely horizon. "Learning to swim wasn't exactly high on my priority list."

He said nothing. Well, what did you expect? she thought angrily. The man had enough relatives to fill a phone book—he could hardly relate to her past as a neglected child. In a moment he'd swim away to join the laughing children, leaving her sitting alone on this dock. It seemed that people were always going away, leaving her behind. . . .

"Would you like me to teach you?"

Laurie's gaze swung back to Gabe. She searched his eyes for some trace of mockery, and found none. "But, I'm too old, aren't I?"

He leaned his elbow on the dock, grinning broadly. "I taught my seventy-year-old grandmother to swim last summer. If she can learn, so can you. Of course," he added, his expression sobering, "you're going to have to learn to trust me."

Laurie bit her lower lip. She didn't exactly relish the idea of placing her life in Gabe's hands, especially after what had happened between them just before they'd reached the reef, but she couldn't see any way around it. His offer was too tempting to pass up.

She'd been alone for most of her life, an outsider in more ways than she could count. But now, at least in this one small way, she had a chance to be like everyone else. She slid off the side of the dock and into the warm water, hanging on to the floating platform with both hands. "Okay, what do I do first?"

"You can start by releasing your death grip on the dock." He swam around to her, coming so close that there was almost no space between them. "Now, put your arms around my neck."

Cautiously she did as he asked—and nearly drowned them both. "*¡Concho!* I didn't mean use your death grip on me," he sputtered, coming up for air. "Wrap your arms around gently—yes, like that. Now, let the water hold you up. It will, I promise. Trust me."

That word again. Since leaving TechniKon she'd trusted only a handful of people, and every one of them had betrayed her. Trust was a luxury she couldn't afford, like seeking a job in the scientific fields she loved, or using her own name. She'd spent the past years looking over her shoulder, always running, always hiding. When she thought about the future, she saw more of the same.

"Relax, will you?"

Gabe's command cut through her imaginings. She saw that he'd swum backward away from the boat, taking them into open water. *Deep*, open water. Suddenly the future seemed much less terrifying than the present. If Gabe left her out here—

"I won't let anything happen to you," he told her softly, as if he'd read her thoughts.

His eyes held hers, their dark surety soothing her in ways words never could. She'd gazed into them before and seen the passion behind his calm exterior. But this time she saw his kindness, and the all-encompassing gentleness that is only found in the strongest of men. She clung to his gaze even as she physically clung to his body, drawing on his whole being for support. Gradually she grew accustomed to the subtle buoyancy of the salt water, and began to work with the sea rather than against it. She reveled in its warm weightlessness, experiencing a freedom she'd never known.

Too soon it was over. Gabe returned to *Dulcinea*, pulling them around to the rear dock. He reached out his hand and caught the edge of the floating platform. "You did fine," he said, giving her a gentle smile.

His simple praise filled her with pride. She knew she hadn't learned to swim yet, or even come close to it, but she'd taken the first step. With Gabe's help she'd managed to overcome one of the fears of her past and, in doing so, changed a part of her future. Maybe, just maybe, she could overcome more. A tightness very much like hope rose in her chest. "Thank you," she said, wishing she could explain the extent of the gift he'd just given her. "Oh, thank you."

He said nothing, but all at once she was aware of a difference in him, and in herself. Suddenly she felt the closeness of their bodies under the water, and the hard strength of the muscles at the base of his neck where she still held him. He was so powerful, so very real. She smelled the warm salt on his skin, saw the drops of water clinging to his impossibly long lashes. She felt his free hand skim down the length of her near-naked torso to her hip, gently pressing her against him. The restraint wasn't necessary—she couldn't have moved away if she tried.

I want him, she thought, struck dumb by the potency of her emotion. But it wasn't only physical—her need for him reached right down into the pit of her being, shattering her with its raw intensity. She'd known him barely a week, yet his dark eyes had branded her soul, making her wish for things she had no business wanting, and ache for a closeness that could only lead to disaster. Caught fast by his gaze she stared helplessly into the mesmerizing darkness, and saw her own uncertainty mirrored in his eyes. Slowly, as if driven by a will stronger than her own, she tightened her arms around his neck, and brought her lips to his . . .

A scream of pain cut the air.

"Adam!" she cried in horror. But it hadn't been Adam. She saw his ungainly orange shape bobbing toward her, towed in by one of the other boys. Relief poured through her, followed quickly by guilt. Adam might be safe, but one of the other kids was in trouble. She scanned the water and saw Jimmy struggling to keep the fourth child afloat. Tony, her mind supplied. The boy who was only a few years older than Adam.

"Get on the boat," Gabe told her.

"But—"

"Do it!" he barked, pushing himself away from the dock. He swam toward the children, his powerful arms slicing through the water. In a few strokes he reached the boys and scooped up the injured child, bringing him quickly back to the boat.

Laurie was waiting on the dock when he arrived. She helped Gabe lift the shivering Tony on board, staring in alarm at the deep red welt that crossed his chest. "What in the world—?"

"Man O' War," Gabe bit out. "Like jellyfish, but worse. Sometimes they come in from the Gulf Stream, but usually not this time of year." In one smooth movement he hauled himself out of the water, then took the child in his arms and carried him to the main deck. He turned to Robert, the boy who'd towed Adam in. "There's some ammonia in the cabin downstairs. Get it."

"Bring a blanket too, Robert," Laurie added. "He's going into shock. It's important we keep him warm."

Gabe gave her a sharp, questioning look. "You sound as if you've seen this before."

"I have," she said quietly. She knelt beside Tony, taking his head gently into her lap. "You're going to be okay, Tony," she said, soothingly stroking his forehead. "Your body's going into shock, but you'll be all right."

"Honest?" the boy said, hope peeking out of his terrified eyes. "You a doctor?"

She hesitated only a second. "Yes, Tony. I am."

Beside her Gabe stiffened. "I know you're trying to help the boy," he said quietly, "but to say such a thing—"

"It's true." She lifted her gaze, meeting his sable eyes with complete candor. She'd just divulged one of her most closely guarded secrets, a part of her past that, if made common knowledge, would help lead TechniKon right to her door. Still, she'd had no choice. The boy was afraid, and fear could ravage a body worse than any wound. She knew what it felt like to be terrified by the unknown, and she'd be damned if she'd let Tony or any child suffer that kind of horror needlessly. She soothed back his wet hair, and looked reassuringly into his eyes. "You're going to be fine," she promised.

Gabe's eyes narrowed suspiciously. "A little young to be a doctor, aren't you?"

"I skipped some grades," she snapped. "Are you going to waste time asking for my credentials, or head this boat toward a hospital?"

She steeled herself for an angry retort. Instead, Gabe bowed to her in old-world deference, then rose to his feet. "You are right—I waste time. When Robert returns with the ammonia, apply it directly to the wound. It will counteract the acid in the sting. But I suspect you already know that."

Without waiting for her answer, he spun around and started toward the tiller, signaling to Jimmy as he went. "Come on, Jimmy. Let's get this boat back to port!"

The trip to the marina seemed to last forever. Robert returned with the ammonia and blanket, then quickly hurried off to help Gabe with the ship. Laurie bathed Tony's welt, grateful that the ammonia did seem to be soothing the inflamed tissue. But the stinger had cut deep, and the boy still moaned and shivered in shock.

Laurie held his hand tightly, trying her best to comfort him. Adam sat by her side, dispensing his own brand of reassurance. "Don't worry," he confidently told Tony. "Mommy won't let anything happen to you."

Finally, they reached the marina. Gabe had radioed ahead to have help standing by, so as soon as the boat docked the paramedics came on board and transported Tony to the waiting ambulance. At least, Laurie assumed that's what happened. By the time the ambulance arrived she'd already taken Adam below deck, out of the sight of the medical personnel and their questions.

She sat on the edge of the bunk and glanced around at the neat, Spartan cabin, trying not to worry about the consequences of revealing her past profession. The curtains could be brighter, she thought, and smiled at the absurdity of the thought. The last thing she needed to be concerned about was *Dulcinea*'s interior decoration.

Gabe entered the cabin, relief evident in every line of his strained face. "They've taken Tony to the hospital, but they think he's going to be all right."

Adam nodded. "Course he is. Mommy's a great doctor."

Gabe looked at her, his eyes brimming with a warmth that made her heart flip over in her chest. "Yes, she is. I owe *you* one for this, *puchunguita.*"

Laurie wet her lips, which had gone suddenly dry. She wanted to believe in Gabe's praise, to trust the sincerity of his gratitude, but years on the run had made her wary. "Did you tell them?" she asked suspiciously. "That I was a doctor, I mean."

Gabe drew back as if she'd slapped him. The relief in his eyes changed to hurt, then anger. His iron control slipped, showing her more starkly than any words how deeply she'd wounded him.

"Gabe, I'm sorry. I shouldn't have said—"

"No, you shouldn't," he agreed curtly. "But you did." He swung around and started up the cabin stairs. "The boys are already in the car. I suggest you come too. That is—" he added bitterly, "if you trust me enough to drive you home."

FIVE

Gabe gave *El Diablo*'s underbelly a healthy whack. Damn, he thought as he poised his monkey wrench for a fresh assault, couldn't this infernal machine stay fixed for more than ten days running? It was barely a week since he was last under this thing . . . the day Yoli had burst into his office with her strange prediction . . . the day he'd first laid eyes on Laurie. . . .

"Damn," he cursed again, aloud this time, and gave the air-conditioning unit another whack for good measure.

"That's not going to help, Nephew."

Gabe craned his neck and saw a pair of impeccably polished Italian shoes standing near his own scuffed Dock-sides. On another day Gabe might have been happy to trade friendly barbs with his uncle, but at the moment he was in a particularly surly mood. A mood that had lasted since last Saturday afternoon.

"*Tío*, when I want your advice on fixing air conditioners, I'll ask for it."

The shoes shifted a little. "I wasn't talking about your air conditioner. I was talking about your golden bird."

Great! Gabe thought darkly. He'd been getting the Dear Abby routine from Yoli all week, and now Carlos was about to chime in as well. Good thing that his secretary was currently out on her lunch break or Gabe would have had to listen to advice in stereo. His nerves were already stressed out from too much work, too little sleep—and a constant sexual frustration that tied his insides up in half-hitch knots.

He pushed himself out from under the air conditioner and sat up, resting his arms on the well-patched knees of his worn jeans as he gave Carlos a baleful stare. "If I have a problem, it's none of your affair."

"None of yours, either, by the looks of it," Carlos commented with a shrug. He sat down in one of the client chairs facing Gabe's desk, blithely ignoring his nephew's murderous glance. "*Válgame Dios*, do you *try* to think up ways to aggravate the woman?"

"Of course not," Gabe said as he stood and walked behind his desk. He slumped into his own chair and pulled an old bandanna out of his back pocket, then began to attack the grease on his hands, rubbing harder than was really necessary. "Besides, what makes you so certain it's my fault?"

Carlos lifted one of his silver eyebrows in wry amusement. He pulled a deck of cards from his impeccable suit coat pocket and calmly began to practice his shuffling technique. "I know you, Gabriel. For years women have swarmed to you like bees to honey. Now you find one who doesn't, and you do not know what to do with her."

He sure as hell knew what he *wanted* to do with her. He'd never kissed her—they'd barely touched— yet just thinking about Laurie made his senses sizzle like a steak on a grill. The back of his neck still burned where she'd held on to him when they'd been in the water, and he could still remember every inch of her sweet, enticingly feminine body pressed against his.

Something unexpected had happened to him in those brief moments, something that made the bankrupt emptiness in his life sparkle and gleam like newly minted coins. When she'd thanked him for the lesson, her indigo eyes had shimmered with a beauty that stole his breath as expertly as his distant relatives had plundered gold.

Startled by her affect on him, he'd pulled away, but the damage had already been done. The curse of his pirate ancestors had finally caught up with him. He knew now what it was like to lust after something so hard and so strong that you'd risk even death rather than lose it. No woman, not even Diana, had ever gotten to him the way Laurie's innocent touches and haunted eyes did. He'd focused on her ripe lips, tempted to do some plundering of his own, and probably would have if Tony hadn't gotten hurt.

And then she'd accused him of ratting on her.

Frustrated, he wadded up the bandanna and stuffed it into his back pocket. "She confuses the hell out of me, *Tío*," he confessed. "One minute she's as trusting as a child, the next she's treating me like something that crawled out from under a rock. It's nuts! She's—Hey, what's so funny?"

"You, Gabriel," Carlos answered, smiling gently. His eyes shone with deep affection for the nephew he loved like a son. "It is good to see you excited about a woman again."

Gabe let out a rasping sigh. Excited? He was *excited* about lots of women, none of whom made him anywhere near as crazy as Laurie. But that, he realized, was exactly what his uncle was getting at. And much as Gabe hated to admit it, Carlos had a point.

Since his fiasco with Diana, Gabe had put a certain distance between the women in his life and himself, keeping a tight rein on his emotions. He governed his deeper passions with an iron will, never losing control of them, not even during sex. The discipline kept him safe and sane, insulated from the violent emotions of despair and betrayal that had nearly torn him apart once before. But it also insulated him from feeling other emotions. Joy. Pleasure. Love . . .

He leaned back in his chair, steepling his fingers under his chin in thought. "Okay, for the sake of argument, let's say I am, uh, excited about her. It doesn't make any difference. She doesn't trust me."

"Bright woman," Carlos said.

"*Tío*—ah, what's the use?" Gabe plowed his hand through his hair, finally giving way to the frustration he felt. "Maybe it's better this way. I don't have time for a woman in my life. And after what happened with Diana, I'm not so sure that I want one."

Carlos stopped shuffling. He gave his nephew a shrewd look, like a poker player gaging an opponent's hand by studying his face. "Is that it? Or do you maybe want this one too much?" He went on quickly, before Gabe had a chance to argue. "I remember when you lost your parents—how you cried yourself to sleep every night for months. You are not a man who loves by half measure, Gabriel. Now I think you are beginning to love something else you fear you might lose, a little golden bird with a wandering nature. You are a grown man, but I think deep inside you there is still that little boy, who remembers how much it hurts to lose someone you love."

He's right, whispered a condemning voice in Gabe's mind. He wasn't afraid Laurie would be like Diana. He was afraid she *wouldn't* be. He'd used the memory of his old lover's duplicity like a shield against another relationship—a very effective shield, until Laurie had come along. But once he looked at it honestly, he had to admit that Diana and Laurie were nothing alike. Selfish Diana would never have burdened herself with the task of loving and raising a child single-handedly. And Diana would never have risked exposure to help an injured child, not even at the height of her deception.

Gabe didn't know why Laurie was so secretive about her medical background, but he intended to find out. Because, much as he hated to admit it, *Tío Carlos* was right about something else too.

Gabe was not a man who could love a woman cautiously, in safe half measures. His corsair blood ran hot within him, demanding total conquest—all or nothing. Considering the intensity of his feelings for Laurie, he suspected he was already half in love with her, and the knowledge gave him no pleasure. For whatever reason, she had, as Carlos so deftly put it, a wandering nature.

Carlos had gone back to his cards. Gabe watched him for a moment, wishing that he could handle his emotions as easily as his polished uncle handled the deck. Carlos gave the cards a few quick shuffles, then dealt out straight kings as innocently as if he were slipping money into a church collection plate. It was a masterful performance, but Gabe couldn't help noticing that there was something odd about the face cards. "Wands, swords, cups . . . Uncle, this is Yoli's Tarot deck."

Carlos swept the kings back into the deck, which he cut with one hand. "Cards are cards," he replied, shrugging.

"Not to Yoli," Gabe warned. "She doesn't like other people messing with them. Something about the vibrations. You'd better put them back before she—"

A shriek from the front office suggested that this option was no longer open to them. Yoli had returned from her lunch break, and apparently she was none too happy to find her cards missing. Carlos, however, didn't seem concerned in the least. "I don't think she'll mind," he said as he rose from the chair and straightened the lapels on his elegant suit. "Especially if I take her out to dinner at the Breakers. It's a good thing I already made reservations."

It was Gabe's turn to give his uncle a shrewd look. "You and *Yoli?*"

"Well, you didn't think I'd come to this godforsaken office just to visit you?" Carlos said, flashing a devilish smile. "Unlike you, I have plenty of time for a woman in my life. Especially one who has a talent for picking trifectas at Hialeah. Wish me luck, Nephew."

"You'll need it," Gabe replied. Some weeks back he'd made the mistake of picking up Yoli's Tarot cards and had almost lost a hand in the process. He didn't envy his uncle's task of taming his feisty, fruitcake secretary. Still, it seemed infinitely easier than trying to slip a tether on his own wild bird.

Carlos seemed to have read his thoughts. Just before he reached Gabe's office door he paused to deliver one final piece of advice. "I've been a gambler all my life, and I know the odds of finding another golden bird like yours are slim to none. The chance for love—real love—comes along only once in a lifetime. I suggest you get yourself over to Berta's store pronto, and give Mrs. Palmer a few good reasons to stay."

"And how do I go about doing that, *Tío?*"

Carlos's grin broadened to sheer wickedness.

"You're a Ramirez, my boy. I'm sure you can figure that out for yourself."

"No, please. You don't have to do this," Laurie said to the lady on the other side of the grocery counter. Her protests were in vain. The stooped woman with the sincere smile absolutely refused to take back the gaily decorated fruit basket she'd just shoved into Laurie's arms.

"Gracias," she said, nodding emphatically. *"Gracias por ayudar a Tony."*

Laurie sighed, reluctantly accepting the gift. From her limited knowledge of Spanish she'd understood that this woman was either an aunt or cousin of Tony. Laurie had tried to explain that she really hadn't done all that much for the youngster, but those protests had been as useless as her attempt to refuse the gift basket. She could have saved her breath.

Laurie turned around and set the basket down beside the pile of flowers and foodstuffs she'd already received from Tony's numerous grateful relatives. *I could have saved a lot of breath.*

"You planning to go into competition with Berta?"

Gabe. She'd imagined hearing his rich baritone so often this past week that she wasn't sure he was real. Guilt over the way they'd parted had distracted her for days. Heated memories of the way he'd held her during the swimming lesson had destroyed her nights. She turned toward him, valiantly trying to ignore the fact that he was even more handsome, more power-fully masculine than she remembered. "Gabe, I . . . what a pleasant surprise."

His sensuous mouth curled into a dubious, yet shatteringly provocative smile. Laurie swallowed, re-membering how close she'd come to kissing him that day on the boat. *And how much she still wanted to.*

Laurie, get a grip! "We're closing in a few min-utes," she stated with a calm she definitely didn't feel. "If you want to buy something, you'd better do it quickly."

Gabe's smile deepened. He said nothing, but there was a gleam in his dark eyes that suggested he'd already picked out what he wanted. Leaning over the counter, he glanced down at Laurie's small pile of gifts. "From admirers, *puchunguita?*"

"You know they aren't," she said, fighting a grin at the man's dangerously contagious charm. Laurie knew he was teasing her—he must have seen Tony's aunt hand her the basket on his way over to the counter. Besides, she suspected very little went on in this neighborhood that Gabe didn't know about. "I wish they would stop it, though."

Gabe's smile lost some of its warmth. "Are you annoyed by their gratitude?"

"No, of course not. Their gratitude means more to me than I can say. But . . . I don't deserve it. I did nothing for Tony."

"Nothing? You took a frightened child and gave him comfort. Without you, he might not have sur-vived. That's not *nothing*, Laurie."

His voice was soft and powerful, like the roll of distant thunder. *He believes I made a difference with Tony,* she thought with wonder. And his belief helped her to believe in herself. "It's just that I hate seeing anyone in pain. . . ."

"I know." He reached out and took her hand, gently enclosing it in his larger one. "I watched you with Tony. You have a gift for healing, a gift that can't be learned from books or classes. It comes from the heart."

He looked down at their joined hands, absently stroking the heel of her palm with his rough thumb. His touch against her sensitive flesh burned through her like wildfire. She felt as if they were back in the ocean, and she was sinking calmly into its warm, lulling depths. If she didn't do something soon, she'd be lost. "I'd better get back to work."

She started to move away, but Gabe refused to let her go. He tightened his grip, drawing her toward him like the relentless pull of the sea. She felt the heat of his skin, the subtle strength of his fingers, the impossible tenderness of his large hands. But most of all she sensed the uncertainty in him, the same vulnerability she'd seen in his eyes when they'd been together in the ocean.

"Why do you hide your gift, *puchunguita?*" he whispered.

His soft words jarred sleeping memories, barely restrained longings. Dream images came back to her, the majestic power of the rising angels, the deadly beauty of the swirling feathers. Something quickened within her, something soft and violent, velvet and lightning. She stood behind an unremarkable grocery checkout counter, surrounded by plantains, pinto beans, and a hundred other ordinary items. But inside, remarkably, extraordinarily, she was falling in love.

No! Gasping, she shook the horrible, wonderful thought from her mind and wrenched her hand from his. "I . . . I really must get back to work."

Gabe's expression barely changed, but the warmth in his eyes died. "Forgive me," he said, his voice edged with sarcasm. "I forgot for a moment that you don't trust me."

His tone, intimate and accusing at once, rubbed her already strained nerves like coarse sandpaper. Suddenly she was angry, at his suspicions, at her silence, at the past that kept her running in circles like a rat in a maze. "Dammit," she cursed, "I don't *like* living this way. And I sure as hell don't appreciate you bringing it up every five—"

She stopped as a hand gripped her arm. Jerking around, she came nose-to-nose with a shriveled old woman wearing an expression that could have turned flesh to stone.

"Diarrhea," the woman challenged in heavily accented English. "You doctor. Fix *now*."

Laurie had received more than her share of threats over the years—from TechniKon, the feds, various lowlifes who tried to take advantage of a single woman on her own. But she'd never gotten an ultimatum from a senior citizen with a bad case of the runs. Despite the tension of the moment her mouth twitched up, succumbing to the deep-seated sense of humor that even six years of living like a fugitive couldn't destroy. Valiantly she struggled to maintain a serious expression, giving the woman a few suggestions to ease her plight . . . until she caught sight of a wicked gleam of amusement in Gabe's eyes.

She burst out laughing.

The elderly woman huffed indignantly, then scuttled away like a crab. The ungainly movement sent Laurie into another fit of giggles. "Oh dear," she said with genuine, if belated remorse, "I've offended her."

"Don't worry. Mrs. Contreras loves to be offended. She'll talk about you with all her bad-tempered friends and they'll have a great time." He pushed himself away from the counter, his brow furrowing with sudden concern. "But it does mean word of your medical skills is spreading. I'll talk to a few people to make sure it stays in the neighborhood." He started to walk toward the door.

"Gabe . . ."

She spoke softly, but he stopped instantly and turned around to meet her gaze. They were yards apart, yet she felt as if he were still touching her, stroking her with a caress that made her feel wonderfully safe and horribly vulnerable at the same time. Everything in her wanted to go to him, to tell him the truth about her past and to hell with the consequences. She couldn't, of course. The stakes were too high.

"Gabe," she said, starting again. "Thanks. For

helping to keep my medical background a secret. Thanks for understanding."

He smiled, but there was nothing warm or humorous in his expression. Slowly, deliberately he walked back to the counter and leaned across it until he was just a kiss away from her lips. "Make no mistake, *puchunguita*. I will find out what I want to know. But not by asking questions."

His eyes narrowed dangerously, studying her with the consuming fascination of a wolf watching its prey. "I won't have to ask," he promised, his voice dropping to a whisper. "Because you'll tell me."

The next two weeks were alternately the best and the worst of Laurie's life. People from the neighborhood kept dropping by the grocery store to see her. Sometimes they brought presents, sometimes they asked her for medical advice, and sometimes they just gave her a nod and a friendly smile. For a woman who had spent her childhood in the cold, impersonal atmosphere of pretentious boarding schools, the simple, uncomplicated friendship offered by her Cuban neighbors was the most precious gift she'd ever received. With the single exception, that is, of one particular Cuban neighbor, whose friendship was neither simple nor uncomplicated.

In fact, he was damn near driving her crazy.

The night after their confrontation in the store, Laurie had a long, sobering, and occasionally tearful talk with herself. She decided she couldn't allow her disastrous attraction for Gabe to continue. She'd put her decision into action the next day and stoically refused Gabe's invitation to take her and Adam to lunch, claiming she couldn't leave the store because she had too much work to do. She hung up the receiver, feeling ten kinds of miserable, but knew she'd made the right—the only—decision.

Her decision and her feelings became moot points a half hour later, when Gabe showed up at the store with an armload of sandwiches. Well, he reasoned, she had to eat anyway, didn't she?

The die was cast. Gabe called up and offered to do something with her and her son, she'd refused, and Gabe managed to get them to do it anyway. He seemed to have a sixth sense for divining what they needed. When the food in her cupboard ran low, a bag of groceries appeared at her door. When Adam heard of a new baby tiger at the Metrozoo, Gabe produced a trio of tickets. For Laurie it was like having her own personal fairy godfather, albeit one who made her blood pressure skyrocket. No one had ever cared about her this much before, and his kindness drew her to him more than his strength or masculine beauty ever could.

Despite his promise that day in the grocery store, he never pressed her about her past. In fact, he never even touched her, treating her with the same well-mannered deference he showed to elderly Mrs. Porra. He told her stories about his own past, from the colorful tales of his nefarious seafaring ancestors, to the more personal, more private stories of his youth. She learned about the death of his parents, and about his nomadic adventures with Uncle Carlos. Cautiously, she shared pieces of her own youth, which had been as nomadic as his, but lacked the anchoring love of a devoted relative. Gradually, as if drawn by the strong and secret undertow of a deceptively calm sea, she began to fall in love.

She knew she was playing a dangerous game. A woman in her situation had no business falling for a man in Gabe's line of work. But while her emotional state was in turmoil, Adam's was brighter than ever. He blossomed under Gabe's influence, making her realize how much her lonely son needed a man in his life. She rationalized the time they spent with Gabe, telling herself that she was doing it for Adam's sake. But in the heart of the night she'd run her hand over the cold, empty side of her bed, and admit that Adam wasn't the only one who needed a man . . . one very special man. . . .

Only, unlike Adam, her needs could destroy them all. If she wasn't careful, Gabe would discover the damning truth—that the boy she loved more than life itself was not her son.

SIX

"What kind of sink?" Laurie asked as she cleared the supper dishes from the kitchen table.

"Not sink. *¡Cinco!*" her son explained in exasperation. "*Cinco de Mayo*. It means the fifth of May, Mexican Independence Day. That's why there's going to be a street carnival. Can we go?"

Laurie stacked the plates into the dishwasher, secretly smiling to herself. She knew about tomorrow night's celebration—*Tía Berta*'s customers had talked of nothing else for a solid week. She'd heard all about the carnival they were setting up in the blocked-off streets of the Calle Ocho neighborhood, with the proceeds going to the local church. *Tía* had even lent her a traditional Mexican peasant skirt, decorated in a bold pattern of bright crimson flowers, for the occasion.

Laurie also knew something Adam probably didn't—that Gabe was the driving force behind the charitable event. Which was why, she assumed, they hadn't seen much of him for the last few days. . . .

"Can we go, Mommy? Can we?"

Dousing her smile, Laurie schooled her features into a stern expression and turned back to her dark-haired son. "Well, I don't know—"

But Adam was already laughing. "You're fooling. I can tell because your mouth's trying not to smile." He climbed out of his chair and threw his arms around her neck. *"Te quiero mucho, Mamá,"* he said in perfectly accented Spanish. "That means, 'I love you very much, Mommy.' Gabe taught it to me."

Laurie hugged him close, knowing that neither the words nor the hug would have been possible if not for Gabe. The man had taught Adam how to show affection to the people he loved, letting him see that there was strength in tenderness. No one could have given him a greater gift. Or her. "Gabe's been a good friend to us both," she said, admitting as much of her feelings as she dared. "I suppose we should ask him to go to the carnival with us."

"I already did," Adam said brightly. "But he's going with someone else. Maria something."

Laurie stiffened. "Maria?"

"Yeah. He told me she was his *amor*, his love. Can I watch TV now?"

Laurie nodded. She waited until Adam left the room, then sank bonelessly onto one of the kitchen chairs. *Maria*, she thought as she absently traced the flower pattern on the tablecloth. *Gabe's amor*.

She shouldn't have been surprised that Gabe had a

girlfriend. She knew enough about the male physiology to realize that men required a certain stimulus that friendship alone couldn't provide. But *amor* suggested something more than a physical relationship. It suggested, she admitted with her uncompromising scientific honesty, something more like love.

Laurie had met dozens of people in her travels, some good, some bad, some downright nasty. But she'd never met anyone who'd shown her the kindness, the unselfish decency that Gabe had. Okay, he wasn't a saint, but he tried to the best of his ability to help the people around him.

It was Gabe's strength and spirit that kept this little Latin enclave from slipping into the bleak decay of the surrounding neighborhoods. His pride in his heritage and his people had restored hope to the community. He had a right to happiness, to be with someone who could give him the love he so richly deserved. Someone who could promise him a future —marriage, home, babies . . .

She couldn't even promise him tomorrow.

Laurie got up from the table and opened one of the cabinets, pulling out the battered coffee can which contained her precious "getaway" fund. The can was full—bursting. It was time, past time, to think about moving on. In the morning she'd go down and tell Mr. Perez, the landlord, that she and Adam would be leaving at the end of the month. No sense in putting off the inevitable. Sooner or later TechniKon would find her, and she'd have to leave anyway.

But as she wiped a lonely tear from her cheek, she

admitted that it wasn't TechniKon she was running from this time.

"Can I have another soda?" Adam asked.

"No," Laurie answered, feeling guilty even though she'd already bought him two. She pressed against the side of the soda booth and pulled her full skirt close to her legs, trying to avoid getting trampled by the close-packed crowd. She hadn't realized that the neighborhood's *Cinco de Mayo* celebration would be such a tourist draw. "I think we should be going."

"But we can't, Mom. We haven't found Gabe yet."

Finding Gabe or, more specifically, finding Gabe and his date, was not high on Laurie's list of priorities. Besides, the crowds were beginning to make her apprehensive. Large groups of strangers made her nervous to begin with, especially when she had Adam with her. With twilight falling, the sea of unknown faces took on dark and sinister qualities. *God only knows who these people are, or who they work for.* Suddenly concerned, she reached down for her son's hand. "We're going home now and that's fin—"

"Laurie," called a familiar female voice. "Laurie, over here!"

She turned in the direction of the voice, and saw Yoli coming toward her. At least, she *thought* it was Yoli. Wrapped in a riot of colorful silk scarves and bangle bracelets, Yoli looked nothing like Gabe's efficient, if somewhat flighty secretary. Laurie's crimson-flowered skirt looked conservative beside Yoli's outfit.

"Laurie, you've got to let me read your fortune," she said as if her life depended on it. "No one's come to my booth for over an hour. It's like they don't think I can do it."

Laurie suppressed a smile, thinking that Yoli's outrageous costume hardly inspired confidence. "No offense, Yoli, but I doubt one person's going to make a difference."

"But it will," Yoli assured her, shaking her bangled head. "If people see me giving you a reading, then they'll want one too. Carlos calls it 'priming the pump,' " she added, as if she were quoting gospel.

Laurie believed in Yoli's fortunes about as much as she believed in Santa Claus, but she couldn't disappoint the older woman. "Okay," she consented. "But make it a short one."

Yoli's face broke into an incandescent smile. "You won't be sorry," she chattered as she led Laurie and Adam through the crowd. "I've been chanting my mantra all this week, and I'm really in tune with the spirits. I'm going to give you a very accurate reading of your future."

Unfortunately, Laurie thought bleakly, *so can I.*

Yoli's booth matched her flamboyant outfit. Purple-and-yellow-striped drapes hung from the sides, while a scarlet canopy surmounted the top. It was tacky in the extreme, yet Laurie had to admit there was a certain allure about it. Not gypsy exactly. Not Arabian Nights, either. She looked at the striped silk hangings and the ropes of fake gold and faux pearls, trying to place her thoughts.

In her mind's eye she saw silk bed sheets strewn with gold coins, beckoning in the flickering lamplight. She felt the prick of a knife against her skin, cutting the confining dress from her body. She felt the cool night breeze whisper against her nakedness, heard the rustle of clothing being shed behind her. She felt hot kisses scorch the back of her shoulders, smelled the brimstone odor of gunpowder, tasted the lusty scent of a man's bare skin—

"Seen Gabe today?" Yoli asked conversationally as she shuffled the cards.

"Er, no," Laurie said, blushing guiltily. Lord, it had only been a silly thought. The dark lover in her fantasy didn't necessarily have to be Gabe. Swallowing, she focused on the cards Yoli was laying out. Anything to take her mind off pirates.

The Tarot cards, however, didn't prove to be much help. "Hmm, the Page of Cups, reversed," Yoli said as she pointed to the first one in the line. "That could mean a deception revealed. And next to it is the Tower, which could mean some kind of trouble coming. And over here is the Lovers. That could mean—"

"Gabe!" cried Adam, and took off like a rocket.

Laurie's head shot up, just in time to see her young son leap into the arms of a broad-shouldered pirate. A pirate! Complete with a flashing saber, a disreputable-looking eye patch, an open white shirt exposing far too much of his muscular chest. For a moment Laurie forgot how to breathe. *The lusty scent of a man's bare skin* . . .

However, the disgusted look on his face was anything but piratical. "This was *not* my idea," he said as he strode up to Yoli's booth. "One of the pirates on the float got sick, and I had the rotten luck to be his size."

"I think you look awesome," Adam said enthusiastically.

"Thanks for the vote of confidence, amigo," Gabe said as he set the youngster down and ruffled his hair. "What does your mother think, eh?"

Adam's mother thought she could use a cold shower. The sight, the size, the smell of him was drowning her senses. She felt like a swimmer caught in a powerful undertow, being drawn slowly and irrevocably under the surface. Drowning had never sounded so good. "It's past Adam's bedtime," she said, trying not to sound as breathless as she felt. "We were just leaving—"

"But I haven't finished your fortune," Yoli protested. "I only got up to the Lovers."

Gabe's mouth curved into a thoroughly wicked smile. "The Lovers?"

Embarrassed heat flooded her cheeks. *Lord, I hope it's too dark for him to see me blush.*

"Why are you blushing, *puchunguita?*"

Laurie winced. The man had eyes like a hawk. Correction—eye. A black patch with a slightly askew band covered his left one, making him look both dangerous and endearing at once. "Damn," she murmured, unable to stop herself. "How did your girlfriend let you out of her sight?"

"My girlfriend?"

"Maria, your *mi amor*. Adam told me," Laurie answered, proud of her composure. No one listening to her voice would guess that her heart was breaking.

Gabe, damn him, had the audacity to look amused. "I think there's been a misunderstanding," he said as he scratched his chin with the tip of his plastic saber. "Maria is *mi amor*, but she's not my girlfriend. She's my grandmother."

"Your grandmother?" Laurie repeated. "Your *grandmother?*"

"Yes, on my father's side," Gabe explained, his expression sobering. As Laurie watched, he pulled off his eye patch and fixed her with the full intensity of his sable gaze. There was no amusement in his eyes now, only warmth, and tenderness, and the boyish uncertainty which had touched her heart so many times before. "I haven't got a girlfriend, *puchunguita*. But, I was hoping you might . . . well, that you might consider—"

He was interrupted by a booming baritone. "Mrs. Palmer!"

Laurie spun around and saw the portly visage of her landlord Manolo Perez waddling toward her. "Mrs. Palmer, I've been looking everywhere for you. I have a couple interested in seeing the apartment."

"Apartment?" Laurie said vaguely, still reeling

from the emotions she'd seen in Gabe's expression. "What apartment?"

"Yours," Perez grunted. "You told me this morning you were leaving at the end of the month. But if you've changed your mind . . ."

"No," Laurie said quietly. She thought about the tenderness she'd just glimpsed in Gabe's eyes, of the hesitancy in his usually confident voice. *I can't even promise him tomorrow.* "No, I haven't changed my mind. You can show the apartment anytime you wish."

Perez nodded and waddled away. Laurie turned slowly, her gaze lighting first on Yoli's disappointed expression.

"You're leaving?" said the gypsy queen.

Adam chimed in. "But we only just got here, Mommy. I don't want to go."

Neither do I, but we don't have much of a choice. She had to get out of here fast, before any other hearts got broken. She raised her gaze to meet Gabe's, and stuck out her hand in an innocuous gesture of goodwill. "Well, I hope you'll wish us luck for the future."

Gabe didn't even look at her offered hand. His eyes, so full of loving warmth a moment before, now sent a chill down her spine. Unconsciously she took a step backward. "I . . . guess we'll be going home now."

"Not until we talk," he stated. He circled her wrist in a grip every bit as uncompromising as his tone. "Yoli, watch Adam for a few minutes, will you? Laurie and I are going to have a little chat."

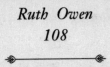

The storage room in the back of Yoli's booth looked like something from the Arabian Nights—on heavy drugs. Only eight by ten feet, it still managed to hold several bolts of tenting material, two aluminum ladders, an assortment of tools used to construct Yoli's and other booths in the area, and a jarringly modern moped.

There were no lights in the room, but illumination filtered in from the outside, between the imperfectly joined slats in the walls. Strips of horizontal light fell across the two occupants of the room, wrapping like ribbons around the contours of their bodies, leaving them mostly in darkness. Gabe watched the strips of light play across Laurie's white blouse and flame-flowered skirt as she entered the room before him. *So much of her is in darkness,* he thought as she moved to the far side of the room. But then, it had been that way from the beginning.

Who are you running from, corazón?

"Why are you leaving?" he asked, hating the harshness in his voice, but unable to control it.

She turned back to him, a thin band of brightness skimming her face as she raised her chin defiantly. "It's a free country. I'm ready to move on. It's as simple as that."

Gabe's mouth twitched up in a humorless smile. If there was one thing he'd learned about his golden bird, it was that *nothing* about her was "as simple as that." She might look as innocent as a baby chick with ruffled feathers, but he was all too aware that behind her ingenuous exterior was a mind as intricate and full of secrets as a treasure map. "And what about the people you've helped with your medical advice—advice you've given freely, without thought of repayment? I've seen you with them. I know you care, whatever you say. There's even talk of setting up a storefront clinic. They need you. *I* need you."

Her chin lost its defiant tilt. "Oh, Gabe. I never meant . . . Believe me, I'm not right for you."

Not right? *Dios mío,* he'd laid awake nights fantasizing about how *right* they could be together. He'd behaved like a bloody Boy Scout around her for weeks, afraid to touch her for fear of unleashing a passion he couldn't contain. Now he realized he might have overdone the Galahad routine. Her words proved that she had no idea of how strongly he felt about her.

But she was going to find out.

He leaned back against the wall, his smile broadening. Slowly he stroked his gaze down the entire length of her body, studying her with an unmistakable male appreciation. "I'm no doctor," he said huskily, "but judging from, uhm, physical observation, I would say you're *plenty* right for me."

He heard the catch in her breathing and knew that, whether she admitted it or not, she wanted him too. "Come here, *cara.*"

She didn't obey. She seemed frozen, caught between conflicting emotions. He could almost feel the struggle within her. Cautiously, like a hunter approaching a wild bird, he moved toward her.

She stepped back. "Gabe, be sensible. You don't know anything about me."

"I know enough," he replied, steadily closing the distance between them. "I know you are generous and giving to those in need. I know you give your son more love in a minute than some kids get in a lifetime. And I know that when I look at you something happens inside me that's never happened before."

This time she didn't back away. Her eyes were in shadows, but a band of light revealed her parted lips, their slight trembling betraying both her uncertainty and her desire. "Why couldn't I have met you years ago?" she breathed.

"You wouldn't have liked me," he assured her. "I was brash and arrogant."

Her lips curved into an incredulous smile. "And you've changed?"

He loved the humor that sparkled out of her at the most unexpected moments. It took a special kind of courage to laugh in the midst of fear, a special kind of woman. An ache like he'd never known began to twist inside him. "Please," he said simply, his clever tongue deserting him. "Please stay."

Her lips, as expressive as her eyes, showed her hesitancy. "No. It's too late. You wouldn't stand a chance against the angels."

"The angels?" he asked, fastening on the clue. "Who are they?"

"Nothing. No one," she said quickly. "Besides,

you're wrong. I'm sorry, but . . . I don't feel the same way about you that you do about me."

"Oh?" he said, his eyebrows arching.

"Yes," she said, starting to move toward the door. "So you see, it's better that I go. But I hope—"

She paused, and looked back at him. A streak of light fell across her face, illuminating her beautiful, too bright eyes. "I hope you find someone who can make you happy. Who can give you the love you deserve."

"Then you feel nothing for me?"

She looked away. "No," she said quietly, heading once more for the door.

She never reached it. He reached out and seized her wrist, pulling her roughly against him. "Prove it."

SEVEN

She came into his arms stiffly, determined to hide the depth of her feelings for him. That resolution ended the moment his lips touched her skin. He kissed her gently, brushing his lips against her temple in an almost reverent caress, cherishing her more than words could say. His touch was delicate, yet Laurie's reaction was anything but.

Raw fire coursed through her, making her ache in places that had no business being affected by a slight pressure on her temple. Intellectually, she knew that medical theory stated that it should take more than one minor caress to bring a female body into full arousal. Apparently medical theory had never figured on Gabe Ramirez.

"We can't do this," she stated, trying to keep her wits about her.

His lips pressed against her brow, and she felt them pull slowly into a smile. "Can't? *Dios*, I haven't been able to sleep nights thinking about the different ways we *can*." He moved to her eyes, dusting soft kisses across her eyelids and the bridge of her nose. "I kept imagining how you'd feel in my arms, wondering if your skin would be silk cool or pepper hot to my touch, whether you'd taste like fire . . ."

"People don't taste like fire," she replied weakly.

"Spoken like a doctor," he chuckled, his laugh a hot whisper against her skin. "Let's find out."

He covered her mouth with his, taking her with such shocking suddenness that she had no time to disguise her true feelings. She melted against him, seduced by the intimate invasion of his questing tongue and the devouring passion of his lips. Everything in her screamed for his heat, his energy, his life. For his love. Her needs, bottled up for six long years, exploded out of her like uncorked champagne. Unable to resist she threaded her fingers through his thick sable hair, and burrowed deeper into his embrace.

"*Dios mío,*" he murmured in wonder. "You're not just fire. You're a volcano!"

His tender words brought her back to reality. She wanted his loving like she wanted her next breath, but she didn't have the right to take it. There was too much he didn't know, too much she couldn't tell him. She lowered her arms and grasped the silky material of his loose shirt as she fought for the strength to stand, and the will to pull away. "We must stop this."

But Gabe had no intention of stopping. His smile curved into a thoroughly devilish grin. "Which *this* do you mean?" he asked innocently. "This?" He brushed his lips gently across hers, sending a jolt of pure electricity coursing through her. "Or this?" He feathered a kiss against an impossibly sensitive spot behind her ear. "Or maybe . . . this?"

He raised his hand and cupped her breast through the thin cotton of her blouse. Expertly he brushed his thumb across the taut, straining nipple. She gasped with ecstasy, and he caught the cry in his own mouth, devouring the sound of her pleasure. The energy she'd always sensed in his soul poured into hers, filling her with his life force, his dark fire.

"You're mine, Laurie, mine," he growled as his tongue ravished the secret corners of her mouth, consuming her with a passion that turned her blood to fire and her bones to water. His hands mirrored his mouth, caressing her sensitive breasts with a skill that robbed her of breath, but made her ache like crazy for more. He was wanton and wicked, a pirate to the core. Yet in the circle of his arms she felt safer than she ever had in her entire life.

This was what she'd longed for during the lonely wandering of the past six years, someone to hold and cherish her, to keep her safe, if only for a moment, from the fearful reality of her pursuers. For the first time in as long as she could remember, she wasn't afraid. She pushed aside his shirt and tangled her fingers in the musky softness of his chest hair, and was rewarded by a deep growl of masculine satisfaction. She loved pleasing him. She imagined discovering his

secrets, and letting him discover the rest of hers, one
by one. All of them . . .

One secret in particular brought her thudding
back to reality.

"I can't," she cried, pushing herself away from
him. Without his arms around her she felt colder and
lonelier than ever. She sank down on the thick bolt of
tenting material, hanging her head in weariness.
"There are things about me you don't know," she
said miserably.

"Like the fact that Laurie Palmer isn't your real
name?"

Laurie's head shot up. "You . . . How did you
find out?"

"It's my *business* to find out." He sauntered over
and set his booted foot on the cloth bolt beside her,
resting his arms across his muscular thigh as he continued. "Your driver's license is a fake. I checked it
out with the state—the number doesn't exist."

"You went through my purse?"

He nodded, his intense gaze showing not an
ounce of regret. "I'd have gone through your apartment if I thought it'd tell me something about you,"
he stated bluntly. Then, bending nearer, he added
quietly, "Would it make you feel better if I told you
I'd have checked up on you even if I wasn't attracted
to you?"

The sudden intimacy, after his roughness, sent a
delicious chill down her spine. He was so dark, so
commanding, so . . . male. She was wildly aware of
him, of the way his leather boot molded to his power-

ful calf, of the hard expanse of his chest, exposed almost entirely by his gaping shirt, of his striped
pantaloons, comically theatrical, yet clinging to him
in a way that left nothing of his lower anatomy—
nothing—to her imagination. He stole her breath.
Dear Lord, I can't take much more of this.

She cleared her throat, and forced herself to look
up at him as if his obvious arousal didn't bother her a
bit. "Did you find out my real name?"

"No." Shifting his stance, he knelt down in front
of her, placing a hand on either side of her. "I was
hoping you would tell me that yourself."

He moved closer, never taking his eyes from hers.
Even in the dimness she saw the uncertainty in his
shadowed eyes, the burning need that even his iron
will couldn't master. When he spoke, his quiet words
seared her soul with buried passion.

"Laurie, I am not your enemy."

She wanted to say that she wasn't sure about him,
that she needed time, but she knew the lie would hurt
him. And she couldn't hurt him, not even to save herself. She lifted her fingers and tenderly touched his
parted lips. "I know you aren't."

His sigh of relief brushed past her fingers like a
prayer. "Thank you for that," he whispered hoarsely.
"Thank you for trusting me."

Common sense warned her to leave. She was falling for this man with the speed of a plummeting me-
teorite, and if she didn't get out of here now it would
be too late to turn back. But she couldn't make her
body obey the command. She was caught like a bird

in a net, held fast by what she saw in Gabe's eyes, doubts and questions she'd seen mirrored too often in her own.

All her life she'd lived apart, separated from others first by her intellect, and later by her fugitive lifestyle. Now she realized that Gabe lived separate too, isolated by his power, his natural strength of command. Impossibly different, they shared a loneliness that had run like a dark river through their entire lives. Until now.

"Oh Gabe," she whispered, filled with a tumultuous combination of joy and helplessness. "What am I going to do with you?"

His eyes sparkled with infernal mischief. "I can offer a suggestion."

He kissed her fingers one by one, laving them with his tongue until the simple act became a potently erotic experience. Laurie moaned, feeling each flick of his tongue echo through her tenfold. His hands followed suit, boldly pushing up her full skirt and stroking her bare legs. He purposely avoided the sensitive area of her inner thighs, sometimes by less than an inch, and the teasing touch brought her to full arousal within minutes. She burned for him, driven by a blood-madness that had never been part of any medical curriculum she'd studied. Wild with need, she went into his arms—and ended up knocking him over and landing spread-eagle on top of him.

"Umph," he said ungallantly. "You're heavier than you look."

"Ohmygod," she said as she pulled herself up his

chest and looked with a doctor's concern into his eyes. "Gabe, I'm sorry. Does it hurt anywhere?"

"Just don't . . ." He paused, drawing in a deep, rasping breath. "Just don't move your leg too quickly, okay?"

"My leg, why—?" She didn't need to say more. Moving slightly, she felt his hard erection press into the soft flesh of her inner thigh. Scant inches higher, her own arousal throbbed into aching, glorious life. "Ohmygod," she said again, for an entirely different reason.

Deep laughter rumbled in his chest. "If you wanted to do it kinky, you only had to ask."

She blushed to the roots of her hair. "I didn't intend . . . that is, I've never done it. Like this, I mean," she finished hurriedly.

"Well, then it's time you did," he said, flashing her a pirate's grin. He circled the back of her neck with his powerful yet gentle fingers and brought her lips down to his. Just before he kissed her, his smile turned serious. "I don't know what you're afraid of, but I won't let anyone hurt you or your son. Not while there's breath in my body."

She gave herself completely to his kiss. In a move that defied physical explanation he reversed their positions, so that he was on top of her, cradling her in his arms. She laughed in surprise, loving his lightning strength, his irrepressible arrogance, his tender yet thoroughly disreputable smile. Wrapped in his arms and passion, she felt his power become her own.

"You're mine," he breathed raggedly, stroking her

lips with hot, moist kisses. "When my pirate ancestors found something they wanted, they claimed it." He moved her body under his, pressing his hot arousal against her aching, empty center. "Feel me," he whispered thickly. "I'm claiming you."

Laurie gasped, feeling the iron heat of him even through the barrier of their clothes. Her hunger for him eclipsed her senses, blotting out everything but the man she loved and her need for him. Cocooned in his dark strength, she felt safe from everything, even TechniKon. They hadn't found her yet. They might never find her in Gabe's insular Latin community. For the first time she really believed there might be an end to the nightmare, and that she'd found a place where she and Adam could live in peace and safety, and love. . . .

"Uh, excuse me," a nearby voice interrupted.

Through the haze of passion, Laurie managed to recognize the figure of Gabe's scarf-swaddled secretary peeping out from behind the storeroom door. *Lord, not now* . . .

"Excuse me," Yoli repeated. "Sorry to interrupt, but you're needed."

Gabe groaned in frustration. "*Concho*, can't this bloody carnival run itself for a couple of hours?"

"Oh, don't be such a bear," Yoli admonished, unimpressed as usual by her boss's ire. "Things are going to hell and back out here. Juan Aguilera has blown out the fuses in three booths with his 'creative wiring,' Anna Del Valle refuses to give the gate receipts to anyone but you, the refreshment stand is running out of hot dogs, and—"

"Enough!" Gabe barked. Sighing heavily, he leaned his brow against Laurie's forehead. "Just give us a few minutes, will you?"

"Okay, but I wouldn't take any longer than that," she warned, shaking her bangled head. "Besides, you two don't have to worry about a thing. Your destiny is to be together. The cards say so."

Yoli vanished in a swirl of mismatched colors, leaving Gabe and Laurie alone once more. The quiet closed around them, but this time Laurie noticed the muffled voices of the people passing by the booth, the slight but undeniable intrusion of the world outside. She hadn't escaped life—Gabe had only put it on hold for a while. The dark cocoon of safety he'd wrapped her in had been an illusion from the beginning. "Maybe it's good Yoli came in when she did," Laurie admitted.

"I don't believe that. I don't think you do either." He gave a long, ragged sigh, then moved off her, his whole body mirroring the regret in his voice. "*Dios mío*, I hate like hell to leave you now. If it were anyone but Crazy Juan Aguilera I would."

"Crazy Juan?" Laurie said, unable to suppress a smile.

"Last month he volunteered to rewire the lights in the church sanctuary. We had to use votive candles to read our prayer books."

He rose and reached down, effortlessly helping Laurie to her feet. The swiftness of the motion caught her off guard, making her stumble against him. Touching him, even this innocently, was almost too much for her to bear. If Gabe were a drug, she'd be an addict. She heard his sharp intake of breath and knew that he felt the same way. "Juan," he commented hoarsely, "has rotten timing."

Outside someone lit a Roman candle. The sudden whoosh of sound made her jump like a frightened colt. But Gabe's firm hands on her arms steadied her, gentling her fright with his unshakable strength and self-assurance. Energy seemed to flow from his hands, soothing her troubled heart and mind. "Don't worry, *puchunguita*. No one is going to hurt you while I'm here."

He meant it. After six years of living like a fox running from the hounds, she'd found someone who wanted to protect her, who was willing to believe in her. Salt tears pricked her eyes. Of all the things he could have told her, none could have been more precious. "Gabe, when you get back, I'd like to talk."

He arched an eyebrow. "We'll do more than talk," he promised with a wicked grin. Then, as if to seal the pledge, he drew her near and placed a gentle kiss on her brow. "My mother used to do that," he told her. "Said it was for luck. I was never sure whether she meant mine or hers."

"Maybe she meant for both of you," Laurie whispered, praying it was true. More than anything she wanted to be a part of this special man's life. And for that she'd need all the luck she could get.

Crazy Juan proved to be the least of his problems.

From the moment Gabe stepped out of Yoli's booth he was accosted by people looking for his help or guidance, a steady stream of catastrophes. He hammered loose boards back into place. He broke up a couple of fistfights, almost receiving a black eye for his trouble. He persuaded a suspected drug dealer to leave the carnival before he personally knocked the stuffing out of him.

Half an hour later Gabe was still dealing with a growing mountain of crises, but he was having a devil of a time concentrating on them. His mind kept wandering back to a darkened room filled with bolts of tent material, cast-off tools, and . . . paradise.

Laurie was his—she'd told him so with every fiery kiss, every breathless cry of pleasure. He ran his tongue across his lips, tasting her sweetness, wanting to taste so much more. He was no stranger to passion, but holding Laurie had given a whole new meaning to the word. He wanted to cherish and seduce her at once—to ravish her with his mouth, and worship her with his body.

Once a pirate, always a pirate.

He grinned at the thought, knowing he'd finally found a treasure worth keeping. She'd fit beneath him as if they'd been made for each other. And the way she'd moved . . . hell, it made him so hot, he swore everyone around him could feel the heat. *Concho, maybe Juan's not the only one who's crazy here.*

Get swept away...

Enter the Winner's Classic Sweepstakes

and discover that love has its own rewards.

You could win a romantic 14-day rendezvous for two in diamond-blue Hawaii...the gothic splendor of Europe...or the sun-drenched Caribbean. To enter, make your choice with one of these tickets. If you win, you'll be swept away to your destination with *$5,000 cash!*

or take $25,000 Cash!

Whisk me to **Hawaii**

CARRY ME OFF TO EUROPE

Take me to the **Caribbean**

Pamper me with **FREE GIFTS!**

GET A FREE GIFT!

Get this personal, lighted makeup case. It's yours absolutely FREE!

NO OBLIGATION TO BUY.
See details inside...

Get Swept Away To Your Romantic Holiday!

Imagine being wrapped in the embrace of your lover's arms, watching glorious Hawaiian rainbows born only for you. Imagine strolling through the gothic haunts of romantic London. Imagine being drenched in the sun-soaked beauty of the Caribbean. If you crave such journeys then enter now to...

WIN YOUR ROMANTIC RENDEZVOUS PLUS $5,000 CASH!
Or Take $25,000 CASH!

Seize the moment and enter to win one of these exotic 14-day rendezvous for two, plus $5,000.00 CASH! To enter affix the destination ticket of your choice to the Official Entry Form and drop it in the mail. It costs you absolutely nothing to enter—not even postage! So take a chance on romance and enter today!

Has More In Store For You With 4 FREE BOOKS and a FREE GIFT!

We've got four FREE Loveswept Romances and a FREE Lighted Makeup Case ready to send you!

Place the FREE GIFTS ticket on your Entry Form, and your first shipment of Loveswept Romances is yours absolutely FREE—*and that means no shipping and handling.*

Plus, about once a month, you'll get four *new* books hot off the presses, *before they're in the bookstores.* You'll always have 15 days to decide whether to keep any shipment, for our low regular price, currently just $11.95.* **You are never obligated to keep any shipment**, and you may cancel at any time by writing "cancel" across our invoice and returning the shipment to us, at our expense. There's **no risk** and **no obligation** to buy, *ever.*

It's a pretty seductive offer, we've made even more attractive with the **Lighted Makeup Case—yours absolutely FREE!** It has an elegant tortoise-shell finish, an assortment of brushes for eye shadow, blush and lip color. And with the lighted makeup mirror *you* can make sure he'll always see the passion in your eyes!

BOTH GIFTS ARE ABSOLUTELY FREE AND ARE YOURS TO KEEP FOREVER no matter what you decide about future shipments! So come on! You risk nothing at all—and you stand to gain a world of sizzling romance, exciting prizes...and FREE GIFTS!

*(plus shipping & handling, and sales tax in NY and Canada)

ENTER NOW TO WIN A ROMANTIC RENDEZVOUS FOR TWO

Plus $5,000 CASH!

or take $25,000 Cash!

No risk and no obligation to buy, anything, *ever!*

Winners Classic

SWEEPSTAKES
OFFICIAL ENTRY FORM

☐ **YES!** Enter me in the sweepstakes! I've affixed the destination ticket for the Romantic Rendezvous of my choice to this Entry Form. I've also affixed the FREE GIFTS ticket. So please, send me my 4 FREE BOOKS and FREE Lighted Makeup Case.

Affix Destination Ticket of Your Choice Here	TICKET	Affix FREE GIFTS Ticket Here	

PLEASE PRINT CLEARLY   CK1   12237

NAME

ADDRESS

CITY   APT. #

STATE   ZIP

There is no purchase necessary to enter the sweepstakes. To enter without taking advantage of the risk-free offer, return the entry form with only the romantic rendezvous ticket affixed. To be eligible, sweepstakes entries must be received by the deadline found in the accompanying rules at the back of the book. There is no obligation to buy when you send for your free books and free lighted makeup case. You may preview each new shipment for 15 days free. If you decide against it, simply return the shipment within 15 days and owe nothing. If you keep them, pay our low regular price, currently just $2.99 each book —a savings of $.50 per book off the cover price (plus shipping & handling, and sales tax in NY and Canada.)

Prices subject to change. Orders subject to approval. See complete sweepstakes rules at the back of the book.

DETACH CAREFULLY AND MAIL TODAY

Don't miss your chance to win a romantic rendezvous for two and get 4 FREE BOOKS and a FREE Lighted Makeup Case!

You risk nothing—so enter now!

FIRST CLASS MAIL

BUSINESS REPLY MAIL

FIRST CLASS MAIL   PERMIT NO 2456   HICKSVILLE, NY

POSTAGE WILL BE PAID BY ADDRESSEE

Loveswept ®

BANTAM DOUBLEDAY DELL DIRECT INC
PO BOX 985
HICKSVILLE NY 11802-9827

NO POSTAGE
NECESSARY
IF MAILED
IN THE
UNITED STATES

Okay, so maybe he *was* a little crazy. Who could blame him? The look of trust he'd seen in her indigo eyes just before he left was enough to send any man over the edge. After weeks of trying to win her over she had finally begun to believe in him. When he finished nailing up this last loose board, he intended to go back to her and sweep her away for a midnight sail on *Dulcinea*. And under the stars he'd tell her all the things he held in his heart, words he'd never said to any woman before. . . .

If I ever get the chance, he added silently, as he watched well-dressed Manny Santos approach him through the crowd.

"We've got a problem," Manny said, possibly for the hundredth time that evening. As the district councilman for the neighborhood, Manny was officially in charge of organizing the *Cinco de Mayo* festival. But unofficially, he hadn't done squat. Like many politicians he was long on promises, but short on follow-through. This event was no exception. "Channel 4 is doing a short piece on the festival, doing candid interviews with the locals, but they need a translator. I told them you'd volunteer."

"Me?" Gabe had dealt extensively with the media during his years on the police force—and had hated every minute of it. Reporters, in his opinion, were at the bottom of the food chain, only a notch above ax murderers and used-car salesmen. "Why can't you do it?"

"Because your Spanish is better than mine," Manny replied, which was true since he barely spoke a word of it. "They've set their cameras up near the playground. Come on, Gabe. The people of this community will thank you—"

"Cut the political crap, Manny," Gabe said curtly. He dropped the hammer and bent down, wiping his hands on his striped leggings. Damn, he wished he'd had the chance to change out of this stupid costume. "I'll act as translator, but that's it for the night. I've got . . . plans."

Leaving the unctuous Manny behind, Gabe threaded his way through the crowd, eager to finish his final job of the evening, and move on to more important things. Important, he thought, shaking his head at the inadequacy of the word. Was a fair wind important to a becalmed ship? Was a buried treasure important to a pirate who'd spent his life searching for it?

Destiny, Yoli'd called it. Maybe she wasn't far wrong. Passionate by nature, he was still ripped raw by the feelings that burned in him when he'd held Laurie. Initially it was the gold in her hair that had attracted him. But it was the gold inside her, her gentleness and generosity, her willingness to help others despite her caution, that drew him to her like a magnet to steel. It was more than lust, more than affection, more than love. Being with her made him feel whole in a way he'd never experienced before. Her gentle fire had reached deep down inside him, and warmed the small, cold corner that had been born on the day his parents died.

Yet someone was trying to kill that fire. . . .

The crush of the crowd increased as he neared the playground. Lured by the chance at temporary stardom, people flocked to the lights and cameras, literally elbowing each other out of the way in an effort to attract the attention of the reporters who milled around the jungle gym. It was sheer chaos.

Gabe's mouth hardened into a grim line. Not so long ago he'd been just as excited about appearing on camera. But that had been before his involvement with Diana, when certain reporters he'd thought were his friends had ruthlessly exposed his very private grief and betrayal, insinuating that he was her partner in crime as well as in bed simply because it made great copy. God, he'd been such a fool.

"Gabe."

Caught up in his painful memories, he barely heard the soft voice at his side. But he felt the pressure on his arm, the gentle touch that would always strike like lightning through his body and soul. Old wounds healed, ancient injustices forgotten. He turned and gazed down into the bewitching indigo eyes of the woman who made him believe in a future beyond the tarnished dreams of the past.

Those eyes were wide with terror.

EIGHT

She didn't say a word. She didn't have to. Gabe's shrewd eyes swept the playground, picking out Adam's familiar form among the half-dozen children on the jungle gym.

"Can you get him?" he asked.

"I'm afraid to go near the cameras," she answered, trying unsuccessfully to keep the tremor out of her voice. Outwardly she appeared relaxed, even calm. Only her eyes and voice betrayed her fear. "Adam was a baby when we left. I doubt they'd recognize him. But if they saw me . . ." Her hand tightened on his arm, rigid with fright. "The angels have spies everywhere."

Angels? Spies? Gabe frowned, feeling as if he'd stepped into the middle of a bad forties movie. But there was nothing theatrical about Laurie's fear. Her terror was very real. He covered her hand briefly, reassuringly with his. "Don't worry, *puchunguita*. I'll get him."

She gazed up at him, her eyes so full of trust it made his heart ache.

"I never meant to involve you in this," she whispered.

"I've been *involved* since the first time I saw you," he said huskily. It was true. Nothing else in his life even approximated the feelings he had for this woman. He didn't give a damn who these mysterious angels of hers were. He only knew he'd die before he'd let anyone lay a hand on her or her son. "I'll get Adam. Then I want you to go to Yoli's and *stay put* this time."

Her mouth turned up in a shaky smile. "Aye, aye, sir," she said softly, her eyes straying to his pirate's costume. "It suits you, you know."

He bent down close to her ear, apparently to whisper something to her over the din of the crowd. But he used the opportunity to press a quick, heated caress on her sensitive lobe. "You have no idea," he murmured.

She watched him saunter away, forgetting, for a full five seconds, how to breathe. The man was an absolute devil, but she trusted him completely with Adam's safety, and her own.

Despite her fear, an absurd happiness welled up inside her. After years of facing her demons alone she finally had someone to take her part, without question, without regret. Someone she could believe in, and who believed in her as well. Someone who needed her love as much as she needed his. *Once Adam is safe I'm going to tell Gabe how much I love him,* she silently promised. *And then I'm going to strangle him for practically knocking my top off with that earlobe thing.*

Craning her neck, she followed Gabe's sable head through the crowd. He navigated the milling throng with an almost unholy ease, utterly confident, never veering from his course. He walked with that same unwavering confidence across the reporter-mined playground, toward the jungle gym, and Adam. Laurie balled her hands into tight fists, praying to God with everything in her to protect both the man and the boy. Her prayers were answered a few moments later, when a small, black-haired child hurtled himself into her arms.

"Adam," she whispered as she hugged the stuffing out of him. "Oh, Adam."

For once Adam didn't fight her embrace. "Gabe said you needed my help. What's the matter?"

"Nothing," Laurie said, brushing away unexpected tears. "Nothing now." Giving Adam a final squeeze, she stood up and searched the crowd for another male she intended to hug the stuffing out of.

But he wasn't in the crowd. He was still on the playground, standing next to the jungle gym. And he was talking to one of the reporters.

Laurie froze. Over the din of the crowd it was impossible to hear their conversation. The reporter was probably asking Gabe something about the *Cinco de Mayo* celebration, but . . .

Stark, windowless room. Cigarette smoke so thick it nearly choked her. So exhausted she could barely hold up her head. Listening while the lab assistants she'd trusted told the angels all about her and Adam.

She swallowed a hard knot in her throat. "Adam, do you think you can find your way back to Yoli's tent from here?"

Her son gave her a look of supreme annoyance. "Of course I can. I'm brilliant."

Laurie bit back a smile. "I forgot," she said apologetically, fighting the urge to give him another hug. "I want you to go there and wait for me."

"Aren't you coming?"

"I'll be along in a minute," she promised, hoping to hell it was the truth. "I want to ask Gabe something first."

Adam seemed satisfied. He started off toward Yoli's tent at his usual dead run. But after a dozen paces he stopped, and flashed Laurie a grin she'd seen many times on another face. A pirate's grin. *"Adiós, Mamá!"* he cried, then disappeared among the sheltering shadows of the tents.

Unexpected tears pricked her eyes. Gabe had given so much to her son, and to her. He was an honorable man in a world that had forgotten the meaning of the word. He'd held her in his arms, surrounded her with his dark strength, promised to protect her and her son. Heat rose within her, burning out her cold seed of fear. Gabe would never betray her. Not after the things he'd said, the way he'd held her, kissed her . . .

But as her gaze strayed back to the two men by the jungle gym, her doubts resurfaced. If the conversation was only a casual one, it would have been over by now. She had to know. Against her will she began to work her way through the noisy crowd, moving closer to the edge of the playground. She wanted to hear what Gabe and the reporter were talking about.

She needed to know if the saint she'd fallen head over heels in love with was really the devil in disguise.

Of all the reporters who could have covered the festival, it *had* to be Carson.

". . . couldn't believe it when they told me you were the translator," Carson said, smiling the boy-next-door grin that had made him one of the most popular newscasters in the city. "Imagine, Miami's legendary police detective living in a run-down barrio."

"This *barrio*," Gabe stated coldly, "is my home. It's where my people live and I'm proud of it."

"Oh, right. You should be," the reporter said, quickly changing gears. "So, have you been in this neighborhood since you left the force?"

Few people would have been astute enough to catch the flash of malicious calculation in the reporter's guileless green eyes. Gabe was one of them. "I agreed to translate for you, Carson, not to give you an interview."

"Sure. But you can't blame me for trying. After the trial you just dropped off the face of the earth. Not that I blame you after what that bimbo did to you."

"She wasn't a bimbo," Gabe snapped without thinking. Then he silently cursed, knowing Carson had found the one chink in his armor. Even after knowing what Diana was, and what she'd done to him, he still could not bring himself to hate her.

"That's right, you were engaged to her. I remember the headlines—Drug queenpin sets police detective fiancé up to take fall. She set you up like a pro." Carson licked his lips, like a hound scenting fresh blood. "You *were* set up, weren't you?"

If they'd been anywhere but an open park, surrounded by people he knew, kids who looked up to him . . .

"I don't want to talk about this," Gabe said, giving the reporter a quelling stare. "Not now. Not ever. Understand?"

Apparently Carson did. Basically a coward, he retreated a step, backing down from Gabe's implied threat. "I'll check if any of the other reporters need you to translate for them. . . ."

Good riddance, Gabe thought as he watched Carson slink away like the dog he was. Unfortunately, the buried feelings the reporter had stirred up weren't so quick to leave. Carson's smarmy innuendos had been irritating, but accurate. Diana had made a fool of him in public, in blazing 22-point headlines. He wasn't surprised that the reporter recalled every sordid detail. The fireworks had gone on for weeks.

Pride, once stripped away, was damned hard to recover. Gabe closed his eyes and leaned his forehead against an iron bar of the jungle gym, feeling the heat of the day still radiating from the metal. His memories of Diana were like that—calm on the surface, but seething underneath like a festering wound. Time had dulled the pain, but not eliminated it.

Diana's duplicity had all but destroyed his faith in others, and in himself. He'd avoided caring relationships, doubting his heart could survive another fiasco. He'd substituted passion for love—fool's gold for the genuine article—and tried to trick himself into believing they were one and the same. *No wonder I never got over Diana*, he thought with a grim smile. *I've been living her lie for years.*

Until Laurie.

She'd washed up on the shore of his neighborhood like an unexpected treasure, touching the lives of everyone with her generosity, her compassion. Touching him with her love. It was crazy to think that something as simple as a kiss could restore his faith in himself, but it had. Suddenly he looked forward to tomorrow, and all the tomorrows after that. He wanted to hold her, cherish her, and, more than anything, free her from the fear that dogged her steps. *Angels* she'd called her pursuers. Who in the hell—?

A flash of gold caught his eye. He turned to look at the milling crowd, instinctively drawn by the color, but found his view blocked by one of the women reporters. "Mr. Ramirez, I wonder if you could translate for me?"

Gabe glanced at the people lining the playground. There were plenty of blondes, but none with Laurie's distinctive red-gold color. Frowning, he followed the reporter, hoping the flash had been a trick of the lights and his imagination. He'd told Laurie to get back to Yoli's, and he prayed that for once she'd obeyed him. He didn't want her anywhere near these cameras, where her mysterious *angels* might see her. He didn't intend for them to find her—at least not until he was ready for them to.

Then, he was going to give them one hell of a fight.

Laurie watched from the shadows as the woman reporter led Gabe away. She didn't think he'd seen her. She hoped he hadn't. Eavesdropping on his conversation with the man named Carson wasn't something she was proud of, especially since it had proved something she should have known all along—that Gabe would never sell her out. Not her. And not, according to Carson, the unnamed woman in Gabe's past.

She set you up like a pro.

Laurie walked away from the congested playground toward Yoli's tent, her head bent in single-minded concentration. Carson had done everything but call Gabe a first-class sap for believing in the woman. Laurie had never considered herself particularly bloodthirsty, but the idea of using that viperous reporter for the stuffing of a king-size burrito suddenly held a lot of appeal.

The playground faded into the distance behind her, but her anger increased with every step. How dare that little wimp taunt Gabe about his past? Gabe Ramirez had more decency in his little finger than Carson had in his entire body.

Gabe had almost single-handedly held this neighborhood together, building a strong, caring community in the center of one of the most crime-ridden cities in the country. He gave his time and energy freely to the people around him, never asking for anything in return. And he'd given her a whole new future full of love and happiness, something she'd never hoped for, even in her dreams.

And what, exactly, are you going to give to him?

Laurie's confident step faltered. My love, she told her conscience, but her intrinsic honesty demanded another answer. She could give him the fear she'd been living with for the past six years. She could give him her police record, making him party to her crime simply by shielding her. She could give him a prime spot on TechniKon's hit list, knowing full well how the powerful conglomerate could systematically destroy careers and lives. Basically, she could ruin his life—another lady who would do him wrong in the end.

Stacked against those odds, love seemed pretty insignificant.

Her steps slowed to a grinding halt. She leaned

back against the side of a booth, wrapping her arms around her suddenly empty middle. Too late she remembered why she'd given up hoping and wishing years ago. It hurt too much when the dreams died.

She couldn't saddle Gabe with her troubles. She loved him too much for that. But she also knew she couldn't tell him the truth. The wonderful, bravehearted fool would probably take on TechniKon single-handed—and lose everything in the process.

The powerful conglomerate would hire a dozen reporters, journalists so slimy they'd make Carson look like a Baptist preacher. They'd rehash Gabe's past in very unpleasant detail, and what they couldn't find out, they'd make up. The angels had never let something as inconsequential as the truth stand in their way before. They'd destroy him with their lies and innuendos. She couldn't let that happen, any more than she could have given Adam to them all those years ago.

She started walking toward Yoli's again, her steps as somber as a funeral march. People she knew passed by her and said *¡hola!*—hello—but she didn't hear them. She was too caught up in her own thoughts.

By the time she reached the fortune-teller's tent she had formed a plan. She asked Yoli to tell Gabe that she had a headache, and that she needed to go home and get some rest.

She took Adam home and put him to bed, but she didn't go to sleep herself. She checked out the bus schedule she kept for emergencies, circling a long-distance flyer that was leaving early the next morning.

She took out the emergency money and counted it, speculating that it would probably be enough to take Adam and herself several hundred miles away from Little Havana. And Gabe.

Pale dawn was just creeping over the eastern horizon when she took a last, poignant look around her small apartment. Adam stood by the door, clutching his stuffed bunny in a death grip, his lip quivering with the tears she'd run dry of hours ago. They'd both been through this drill many times in many years, but Laurie knew that, for both of them, this time was by far the hardest.

Laurie picked up the suitcases and started down the deserted hallway, keeping her steps as quiet as a cat's. She'd left a note for Mr. Perez on the counter, along with a couple for Berta and Yoli. She'd tried to write one to Gabe, too, but that had proved impossible. Words couldn't begin to express the depth of what she felt for him. Besides, her tears kept falling on the page, blotching the ink.

She heard the faint honk of a horn, and knew that her taxi waited below. It was time. With Adam beside her she reached the top of the staircase. She glanced one last time at the narrow hallway, and her apartment door. It was impossible not to remember that first night, when Gabe had walked her home from Shanghai Bill's.

I fell in love with him then, she realized. *I looked into his strong, sad eyes, and fell in love with him.*

New tears pricked her eyes, an impossibility after

the amount she'd already shed. Sniffing, she wiped her eyes on her sleeve, and started down the first step.

She never made the second. Steel fingers grasped her arm, and a voice she'd expected to hear again only in her dreams asked, "Going somewhere, *puchunguita?*"

NINE

They needed to talk, and the only place they could speak in private was Laurie's bedroom.

Gabe walked in first and set down the suitcases that he'd taken from her in the hallway. Then, without a word, he flopped onto her bed. He linked his hands behind his head and relaxed comfortably on the pillows as he watched her intently. The old bedsprings groaned, unaccustomed to his weight. Laurie groaned too at the sight of his lean form stretched so casually on her bed, but for an entirely different reason.

"I wish," she said with some effort, "you wouldn't do that."

He grinned, but his smile didn't reach his eyes. He crossed his long, jean-clad legs at the ankle, an effortlessly sensual gesture that sent her temperature shooting up a full ten degrees. "This bothers you?

I'm surprised . . . considering how little last night must have meant to you."

"That's not true! It meant . . ." she began, but her words dwindled off. What could she say to him? That last night had been the most precious moments of her life, but she still had to slink off like a thief in the night? He wouldn't believe her. Hell, she wouldn't believe it either.

He thought she had betrayed him, just as that woman in his past had. The knowledge cut through her heart like a jagged knife. She turned to the window, feeling the fresh sting of tears in her eyes. "You don't understand," she said hoarsely.

"I understand more than you think," he replied.

There was no warmth in his tone, only anger, and bitterness. *Dammit, I can't bear hurting him anymore.* She whirled around, determined to tell him the truth and to hell with the consequences. But he wasn't looking at her. He was staring at a sheet of fax paper he'd apparently just pulled from his back pocket.

"After Yoli gave me your message I went back to my apartment. But I was more in the mood for . . . well, not for sleeping. Finally I gave up and went to the office. I thought," he added, his smile turning grim, "that I'd get some paperwork out of the way, so we could spend the day together."

"Gabe—"

"Save it," he said harshly as he tossed the paper onto the side of the bed nearest her. "When I got to the office I found this on the fax machine. I suggest you take a look at it before you say anything else."

Laurie picked up the crumpled sheet. The light of the new dawn filtered through the window behind her, illuminating the page with golden fire. But the words printed on it were the ashes of her old life, sour and smoldering, refusing to die. *Dr. Margaret Lawrence, former associate director of Genetic Research at TechniKon Industries, wanted for grand theft, industrial espionage, treason . . .*

A small picture accompanied the text. The woman it depicted was twenty pounds heavier than Laurie, and wore a determinedly somber expression, as if smiling was an unnecessary indulgence. It was like looking into a carnival mirror, where the image is warped out of focus, obscenely distorted.

The scientist in Laurie automatically examined her feelings, the uncomfortable meeting of her past and present. There was no mistaking the strong line of her jaw, the unusual shape of her eyes, the strangely wistful expression in the no-nonsense face. Dr. Margaret Lawrence was the woman she used to be.

During the past twenty-four hours Laurie had been buffeted by dozens of feelings, everything from passion, to fear, to despair. Discipline and love for Adam had held her together until now, but the old photo was too much for her to bear. Her insides seized up like an overloaded electric circuit. Emotionally, she switched off.

"I hate this picture," she said numbly. "Of all the pictures they could have used, why this one?"

She didn't know how long she stood there, staring

at the paper. She didn't hear Gabe leave the bed and walk over to her. She barely felt it when he took the sheet from her hand, and wrapped her in his comforting arms. He drew her back to the edge of the bed, cradling her in his lap like a frightened child. "That is so like you, *cara*," he sighed. "Up to your pretty little neck in trouble, and you're worried about an old picture." He gently stroked her hair, as if he was unable to make his body obey the sternness in his voice. "So what do I call you? Margaret? Dr. Lawrence?"

"Laurie. I've been called Laurie ever since I was a child." She rested her head against his shoulder, the icy numbness inside her thawing just a little. "I meant to tell you. I wanted to tell you so many times, but—"

"But you were afraid I'd turn you in," he finished.

"No!" Laurie looked up in surprise. She met his gaze, unable to ignore the anguish and self-reproach in his eyes. With a start, she realized his anger was directed against himself, not at her. "I know you'd never turn me in. I've known it for a long time."

Gabe laughed hollowly, clearly disbelieving her. His sable eyes, once alive with dark fire, grew as cold and empty as the space between the stars. Despite his nearness Laurie felt him slipping away, retreating to the isolation of his past, the separate loneliness. Lord knows how long it would be before he let himself get close to another person again. If he ever let himself get close.

She couldn't let that happen. He meant more to her than her freedom. More, she realized, than her life. She grasped his shirtfront, seeking purchase in the soft cotton which covered his solid chest, and began to tell him the story she'd spent six years trying to forget.

"Like the paper says, I was employed in the Research and Development Department of TechniKon Industries as a genetics engineer. I was part of a team working on an experiment based on the Human Genome Project—"

"The what?" Gabe asked.

"Human genome. The mapping of the human chromosome, gene by gene. Scientists hope to discover the genes that give a person blue eyes or brown, or, more importantly, Alzheimer's or cancer. It's an incredibly complicated process and several international corporations are spearheading the effort."

"Like TechniKon?" Gabe supplied.

Laurie nodded. "TechniKon is a major player. The government awarded them huge research grants on a regular basis—and not all of the money went to the assigned projects. Corporate officers' bank accounts got awfully plump. But even that wasn't enough for some of them. They wanted more, and they didn't care how they got it."

Unconsciously Gabe pulled her closer, as if to protect her. "Like the drug dealers I came up against on the force. Greedy dogs who would have sold their own mother for the right price."

"Yes, they're like that," Laurie whispered, remembering TechniKon's CEO, a silver-haired man whose politician's smile hid a cruel and vicious nature. "I found out that they were going to sell my project to a

foreign power, a nation long on wealth and short on
human rights. I knew that country would misuse h—
the experiment, so . . ." She lifted her chin and met
Gabe's gaze squarely. "So I stole it. I stole all the
research, too, so they couldn't recreate the project.
Then I ran."

For a long moment Gabe said nothing. He simply
held her, letting her absorb the strength of his arms,
the surety of his beating heart. For years she had been
running on quicksand, never daring to rest for fear of
being sucked down into oblivion. But pressed against
Gabe's rock-hard body she felt safe, protected from
the dangers which surrounded her.

Last night she'd given him her passion. This
morning she'd given him her trust. She closed her
eyes, wishing there was some way on God's green
earth that she could stay with him without exposing
him to TechniKon's vengeance. But of course there
wasn't. The laws of the state were as unyielding as the
laws of nature.

She started to push herself away from his chest.
"So you see," she reasoned with scientific logic, "I
have to go."

Gabe's iron arms locked around her. "I see nothing of the sort. TechniKon is the criminal, not you.
We can take them to court—Uncle Carlos can repre-
sent you. He may not look it, but that wily old man is
one of the best lawyers in the country. He'll get you
the justice you deserve, maybe even get the media
involved—"

"No!" Laurie cried. "You can't . . . Gabe, I don't want the papers to get hold of this story."

"Why not?"

She stared at him in silence, desperately trying to formulate an answer that would satisfy him without giving away too much. For one crazy moment she considered telling him the truth—the whole truth. Then she heard muffled sounds coming from the living room, where Adam was watching cartoons. Watching cartoons, just like any other six-year-old.

"Gabe, I won't go to the media, or to court," she said resolutely. "I . . . have my reasons."

"Reasons you have no intention of telling me about," Gabe finished in his stern baritone. "Am I right?"

She nodded, feeling more miserable than she'd ever imagined she could in his arms. "I told you last night that I didn't want to get you involved in my problems."

"And I told *you* that I am involved."

The morning sun pooled in his eyes, making them burn with raw fire. At least, she hoped it was from the sun. Just being near him made her insides bubble like hot, sticky caramel. A minute ago her numbness had protected her, but now her senses were returning, and with them sexual awareness. It was impossible for her to be this close to him and not want to run her hands over his hard flesh, to focus on his sensual lips without wanting to kiss them, to smell his intoxicatingly male scent, and not want to—

"Will you at least promise me that you won't leave without talking to me first?" he asked quietly.

I love the way you talk, she thought foolishly. *I love the way your hair falls over your forehead, and the way the corner of your mouth twitches up when you're trying not to smile. I love the way you always try to take care of people, even when it's not the smart thing to do. I love that you think you can make a difference, even when you can't. I love you, Gabe Ramirez,* she finished silently. *And the best way I can prove it to you is to get out of your life forever.* "I promise."

For a long moment he studied her face, fixing her with the relentless stare that had made him a first-class private investigator. She met his gaze squarely, knowing that her secrets were too deep for even him to fathom. She fully expected him to ask more questions.

She didn't expect him to throw back his head in a shout of laughter.

He tumbled her off his lap and onto the bed, then scooted over to the bedside table and the phone. Still chuckling, he picked up the receiver and quickly punched in a number. "Yoli? Good, you're there. Listen, I want you to bring the bag I keep packed at the office over to Laurie's apartment . . . yes, you heard me right."

He spoke a few more sentences, all in Spanish, then set down the receiver. Grinning like a Cheshire cat he leaned back against her pillows, in the effortlessly sexual pose that had set her blood simmering to begin with. He looked up at her stunned expression, his own face betraying not one ounce of remorse. "You know, *puchunguita*, one of the things I love best about you is that you are such a poor liar."

The lady could give lessons to clams, Gabe thought ruefully as he watched Laurie put away the last of the supper dishes. Since their conversation this morning she'd spoken barely a dozen sentences to him, giving curt answers about where to put his unpacked clothes, or asking him what he wanted in his coffee.

To her credit, she made things comfortable for him. She'd given him closet space to hang his clothes, and even made up the living room couch as a bed. But he wasn't fooled by her hospitality. The furtive expression in her eyes told him she still had every intention of running as soon as his back was turned.

Dammit, puchunguita, can't you see I'm only trying to help you?

Although Laurie was giving him the silent treatment, Adam more than made up for it. He'd shown Gabe every toy, every game, every book in the apartment. Currently he sat beside Gabe on the couch, explaining the dubious virtues of something called "Monster Slime." Gabe smiled broadly as the youngster used incredibly technical terms to describe the incredibly untechnical green goop. The kid had a lot of his mother in him.

He'd always been good with children—his pack of young relatives worshiped him like a god—but

Adam's friendship meant more to him than all the rest of them combined. Perhaps it was the boy's unusual intelligence, or the haunted look that sometimes crept into his expression, just as it crept into his mother's. Or perhaps it was because Adam was Laurie's son, the child of the woman he wanted for his own.

Much as he liked children, Gabe had never given much thought to having one of his own. His relatives and the neighborhood kids had always satisfied whatever paternal needs he had. Yet being with Laurie and her son, watching the affection they had for each other, made him yearn to be part of their tight, loving family. He realized that he not only wanted a child, but that he wanted to make one with Laurie. He flushed hot, imagining what it would be like to know that his own seed was growing in her belly.

Of course, first he had to convince her to stay.

Laurie called from the kitchen, interrupting his thoughts. "Adam, it's time for bed."

The boy made a plaintive sound designed to cut straight to the heart. "Aw, can't I stay up a little longer?"

"No, you cannot," his mother stated. She entered the living room, wringing out a dishtowel in a very no-nonsense manner. "It's already an hour past your bedtime. Now give me a hug good night, then go and get into your pajamas. I'll come tuck you in, in a few minutes."

"Aw," Adam grumbled again, but he walked over to his mother and gave her a heartfelt hug. He started to leave the room, but instead dashed over to give Gabe an impulsive hug. "I'm glad we didn't leave this morning," he confided. "And I'm glad you're staying with us." Then he turned on his heels and left the room before the touched and startled Gabe could think of a thing to say.

After Adam left, the room fell into a charged silence. Laurie stood halfway across the room, facing away from him, yet Gabe felt connected to her in every sense of the word. He imagined he could feel her heartbeat, hear her quickening breath, touch the red-gold tangle of her hair as it slipped through his fingers. It had been said that his pirate ancestors could sense the hidden treasure on an approaching ship as soon as they caught sight of her sail. He knew now what that felt like.

"Adam is very fond of you," Laurie said quietly.

"I'm very fond of him," Gabe answered, wishing she would look at him. Then, praying he wasn't taking a fatal misstep, he added. "The boy needs a home."

He got his wish. Laurie spun around and looked at him. More precisely, she *glared* at him. "He has a home."

"He has suitcases and rented rooms," Gabe countered as he rose to his feet. His common sense warned him that he would probably regret this, but at the moment he didn't care. Love, lust, and worry had pushed him dangerously close to the edge. "Skipping from town to town, trading one empty name for another—what kind of life is that for a kid?"

Laurie's eyes blazed. She lifted her chin, staring at him with the haughtiness of a goddess. She wore a faded cotton dress, held a wet dishtowel in one hand, and unsuccessfully tried to smooth back her electric tangle of hair with the other. Her appearance was far from remarkable, yet the aura of magnificence that surrounded her took Gabe's breath away.

"We'll get by," she stated with icy surety. "Besides, we don't have much of a choice."

"Yes, you do." He began to walk toward her, his powerful strides accenting each word. "You need a name, I'll give you a name. Mine."

She didn't move a muscle, but her face went pale as a ghost's. "That's . . . that's very kind of you, but—"

"Kind!" Gabe roared. He gripped her shoulders, barely containing the urge to shake some sense into her. "Kind is the last thing I'm being. *Dios*, woman, don't you know what you do to me? I can't think for wanting you. I dream about you at night, and wake up so hard, I can't breathe. I want you and Adam to be a part of my life every day, every hour. I don't care who you are or what happened before I met you. I only know that I love you."

He'd expected her to fall into his arms. Instead, she stared at him in shock, as if he'd just confessed to a murder. "Well," she said evenly, "I'm sorry, because . . . I don't love you."

"Liar," he said, pulling her to him. He kissed her thoroughly, hungrily, consuming her with the fire that raged through his own soul. He thrust his tongue into the vulnerable heat of her mouth, taking her with a mastery that made her moan with pleasure. She melted against him, completely undone by the fierce desire of his kiss. Within him, a spark of hope began to glow to life. But when he reluctantly lifted his head from hers and gazed into her eyes, that hope died. Her skin was flushed and her lips were swollen with lush passion, but her eyes were as empty as a shipless horizon.

"Just because I respond to you physically doesn't mean I love you," she said with killing calm.

Gabe stepped back as if she'd slapped him. Instinct told him she was lying, but he couldn't be sure. Love and passion were two sides of the same coin, yet it was all too easy to mistake one for the other. He would have sworn on the Holy Mother that Laurie loved him as deeply as he loved her. But then, he'd thought the same thing about Diana.

"Mommy? Aren't you gonna read me a story?"

Adam stood in the entryway between the hall and the living room, dressed in his Batman P.J.s. He glanced with shining innocence at the two adults, completely unaware of what had just taken place between them. Gabe swallowed, feeling a horrible tenderness tug at his heart. How long can Adam's innocence last without friends, without a home, without love . . .

Laurie went over to her son and shooed him through the entryway. Then she glanced back at Gabe. "You . . . I'll understand if you decide to leave. There's no reason for you to stay anymore."

She turned away, resting her hand on the doorjamb as she added, "I'm sorry." Then she was gone.

Slowly Gabe walked back to the couch. He sat down heavily and ran his hands over his face, exhausted in a way he'd never been before. He'd figured out a dozen ways to help Laurie and her son, but they all depended on her loving him. With that vital piece missing, the whole tower fell in on itself like a house of cards.

The pirate in him urged him to claim her despite her objections. The private investigator in him told him to keep digging, that there was much more here than met the eye, even if Laurie insisted there wasn't.

But there was a part of him, lonely and cold, that felt as if he'd just lost his parents all over again.

TEN

The sound of wings.

Once again she was running from the angels, feeling the wind from their beating feathers hammer her skin like a hurricane. She ran until she couldn't breathe, until her heart pounded so hard, she thought it would burst through her chest. She ran until she was past the point of exhaustion, until her legs turned to lead and her bones to water. But it was worth it. For the first time she felt the infernal wind lessen, and she knew that she had finally found the strength to outdistance her pursuers. She turned around, ready to shout in triumph.

Then she saw why the angels had stopped following her. They were chasing someone else, a dark man whose magnificent strength was still no match for the angels. She watched helplessly as they closed in and surrounded him with their cutting, killing feathers.

"No," she moaned, struggling toward waking. Yet

her fear increased as consciousness returned. She physically felt the angels' hands grip her, holding her back from Gabe, keeping her from saving him, or dying with him—

"Laurie, *cara*, it's all right. It's only a dream."

Gabe. Her eyes flew open and she found herself looking up into the face of the man she loved. With a cry of relief she wrapped her arms around him, hugging herself against him like a second skin. "You're safe."

"*I'm* safe?" She felt his hard muscles shift as he pulled her into his lap. "*Dios*, what were you dreaming about?"

"The angels," she whispered, too relieved to lie. She burrowed against the warm comfort of his chest, innocently grateful that he was naked from the waist up. His jean-clad legs rubbed coarsely against the bare skin of her thighs, but she didn't care. She just burrowed deeper, held on tighter.

"The angels are TechniKon's security guards. They wore white lab coats—that's how they got their nickname. Kind of a sick joke." She rubbed her cheek against the crisp, musky-smelling pelt that covered his chest, breathing in the reality of him. "But they weren't chasing me this time. They were after you. I was so scared."

"You were scared for me?" he said, tightening his arms around her.

"Horribly," she admitted, lifting her gaze to his face. In the darkness she could see only the shadowy outlines of his profile, but she could feel the strength of his arms, the buried vibrancy that radiated through his body like the energy of a dark sun. He was real. He was safe.

But for all his wonderful strength she knew he was made of flesh and blood, like any other man—vulnerable, mortal. A sitting duck. Her breath caught in her throat. "If anything happened to you, I—"

"Shh, hush," he said as he pressed a moist, gentle caress against her temple. "I'm a big boy, *puchunguita*. I can take care of myself."

"No, you can't," she stated as the cold, deadening fear seeped back into her. "TechniKon plays for keeps."

The light of a flickering streetlamp cut through the darkness, catching the gleam of his smile. "So do I."

Afterward, she was never sure who kissed who. They met halfway, Laurie raising her head to meet Gabe's descending lips. Their mouths joined in a fiery dance that fused them together, searing them both from the inside out. He tasted her deeply, lavishly exploring her most tender recesses, enticing her to do the same. Laurie felt places inside her she didn't even know existed blossom into lush, throbbing life. Gabe's power poured through her, filling her with a hunger that increased with every frantic beat of her heart.

He spun a dark spell around her, taking her small cries into his own mouth, and giving them back in throaty, carnal moans. He threaded his strong fingers through her hair and pulled her close, binding her to him. Yet she yearned for another joining—wilder, deeper, more savage . . .

Then, without warning, he tore his mouth away from hers. Breathing raggedly, he lifted her from his lap, then rose unsteadily to his feet. "It's no good," he said hoarsely, shaking his head in despair. "Friendship and caring . . . it's not *enough.*"

She didn't know what he was talking about. She didn't care. Her whole body screamed for his touch. Nothing mattered except Gabe—not TechniKon, not the angels, not even the fear that had defined her life for so many years. She just wanted Gabe to hold her, to touch her and to take away the awful, aching emptiness inside her. "Gabe, please," she said, her voice thick with longing. "Please, stay."

She reached out and lovingly stroked his muscular forearm. He jerked away as if she'd touched him with fire. "*Concho,* you tear me apart! Last night your kisses promised me a lifetime of loving, then this morning I find you slinking away without so much as a good-bye. Tonight you want my love, but what about to-morrow? Will I find your side of the bed cold, your suitcases gone?"

"I . . . don't know," she whispered. "I honestly don't know."

"That's just not enough," he repeated, his words an open wound. He touched her cheek briefly, like a prayer, like a farewell. Then he disappeared into the shadows that cloaked the bedroom doorway. In the silence, she heard the door close with a final, damning click.

She couldn't breathe. Regret choked her, regret for a future that could never be, a life she would never share with this brash, sexy, impossibly dear man. She drew up her knees and wrapped her arms tightly around them, as if by making herself smaller she could lessen her sorrow. It didn't work, of course. As a geneticist, she knew that species' chromosomes remained basically the same, no matter what physical shape she twisted them into. Sorrow, it seemed, followed the same rules.

A sob rose in her throat, bringing with it the words of truth that she'd denied for far too long. "I love you," she breathed into the unheeding darkness. "God, I love you." Then she laid her head against her knees and began to sob in earnest.

With her senses diluted by the tears, she wasn't aware of him until she felt his hand on her shoulder. The light touch shot through her like an electric shock. She jerked back to the far end of the bed, crouched for battle, her emotions shifting from despair, to surprise, and red-hot anger at the speed of sound. It took her just a second to figure out that he'd closed the door without leaving the room, that she'd been duped by a trick that even six-year-old Adam wouldn't have fallen for. "You bastard!"

"A bastard and a liar," he commented pleasantly as he settled himself on the thick pillows piled against her headboard. He linked his hands behind his neck and stretched out like a well-fed panther. "A good match, I think."

"Get out of my bed!"

"Careful, *puchunguita*," he said with patently false concern. "You'll wake your son."

"Adam can sleep through anything," she said sharply. Too late she realized what the words implied, and hoped he'd miss the double meaning.

He didn't. Gabe shifted his lean body, his white teeth flashing in the darkness as he smiled. "Anything?"

"That's not . . . ooh," she said, boiling with frustration. She turned her back to him, hunkering down in a childish and extremely satisfying gesture. "I want you to go."

"No you don't." The bedsprings squeaked as he slid up behind her and hovered tantalizingly close to her body. "You love me."

"I don't. I can't," she said, but her resolve weakened as she felt the heat of his breath against the sensitive base of her neck. "Gabe, I can't let this happen."

"It already has." He pushed her loose T-shirt down her arm and placed a slow, wet kiss on her bare shoulder. "It happened the first time I saw you, when the sunlight lit your hair like a shower of gold." He trailed sweet, searing kisses across her skin to her ear, then stopped her breath as he sucked the tender lobe with wicked playfulness. "Since that moment there's been no one else. You're my golden desire, my precious treasure."

"No," she said hoarsely, fighting the tidal wave of heat rising within her. He'd managed to slip his hands under her nightshirt, and somehow she couldn't summon the strength or the will to stop him. Warm hands caressed her stomach, and slyly worked their way toward other areas. She bit her lower lip, using the sharp pain to clear her head. Dammit, *somebody* had to be sensible. "I'm not a treasure. I'm a fugitive on the run. I'm a criminal, Gabe, just like—"

His questing hands stilled. "Like who?"

"No one," she said quickly, silently praying Gabe would be satisfied with the answer. She prayed in vain.

A low, feral growl rumbled in his throat. Without a word he pulled her to him, flattening her back against the hard wall of his bare chest. He lowered his mouth to the pulse point in her neck, and performed a series of maneuvers with his tongue that would have been banned in Boston. When she was thoroughly and completely undone, he lifted his mouth to her ear, caressing her with his breath as he repeated his question. "Like who?"

Lying was no longer an option. "The woman in your past who almost ruined your life," she breathed, amazed that she got the words out when there wasn't a cubic inch of air left in her lungs. "I heard you talking to Carson."

"Carson," he hissed, his tone making the name a curse. "The man is *despreciable*—trash. He wouldn't know the truth if it ran over him in a powerboat."

"He was telling the truth about that woman." She rested her head against his shoulder and looked up into his eyes. "You got mixed up with a criminal before, and it almost destroyed your life. I don't want to put you through that hell again."

"Ah, Laurie," he sighed. For a long moment he stared into the darkness, just holding her, saying nothing. When he spoke his words came slowly, as if they'd been bottled up in him for a long, long time. "When I was on the force, I ran with a fast crowd, the beautiful people of the city. Even among that bunch Diana stood out, like the star on an overdecorated Christmas tree. I was green enough to mistake her glittering false love for the genuine article, and I paid for it."

"She hurt you," Laurie said, lifting her hand to stroke his beard-roughened chin.

Under her fingers, his mouth pulled into a smile. "Not as much as I hurt myself. I nursed my pain, letting it fester inside me. I never let anyone get close to me, never allowed myself to care for anyone deeply, until . . ." He looked down at her, his voice blurred with laughter. "Until a little golden bird knocked me on my ass."

"That wasn't my fau . . ." she began, but her words died in a strangled gasp. Gabe's hand covered her breast, rubbing the rough pad of his thumb against her pebble-hard nipple. Thick, molten lava crept through her veins, pooling like liquid fire between her legs. Whimpering, she inched closer to him, and felt his hot erection pressing against her backside.

"Feel me, *puchunguita*," he whispered as he caressed her ripening breasts. "Feel how much I need you."

If he'd used a word other than *need*, she might have been able to resist him. But she loved him too much to deny him, too much not to give him whatever peace he could find in her heart and body. Last night she'd sensed the emptiness in him—tonight she'd learned the reason. They'd both been running from the past—running so hard that they'd almost missed this precious moment, this glory that flowed between them like a golden river. *I can't promise him tomorrow but, by God, I can give him tonight.*

She turned in his arms until she faced him, staring boldly into his dear, dark eyes. "I need you too," she admitted. Then, feeling like she was stepping off the edge of a cliff, she added, "I want to make love with you. But there's something I have to tell you first—"

"Damn right there is," he growled.

His arms tightened around her, pulling her into the vee of his legs and against his hard sex. His jeans and her silk panties offered little protection against the shock of heat that sizzled through her like lightning. She moaned, mesmerized by the feel of him pulsing against her soft, barely protected center. The words she'd meant to say to him tumbled out of her mind like apples from an overturned barrel.

"Say it," he demanded with silken softness. "You said it to the darkness, but I want you to say it to me. Tell me you love me."

"I love you," she said willingly, without so much as a moment's hesitation. And with those simple words a dam broke in her heart. The love she'd denied for so long poured out of her in a thundering torrent of emotions. She curled herself around him, wanting to prove her love with every part of her. Touching him became as necessary as breathing. She feathered hot, sweet kisses across his chest, feasting with delighted hunger on his body. "I love you with all my heart."

"And I love—*Dios!*" He gasped as she expertly laved her tongue against one of his nipples. "Where did you learn that?"

"I'm a doctor," she said, glancing at him slyly. "I'm fully knowledgeable about all the male erogenous zones. Female ones, too, if you want any sugges . . ." Her words dissolved into a desperate squeak as he stroked a part of her that she'd never considered to be the least bit erotic—until now. "Forget what I said about suggestions," she finished breathlessly. "You don't need any help."

"But I do, *puchunguita*," he answered, his voice sobering. He fanned his hand across her throat, using his thumb to raise her head to meet his midnight gaze.

She saw the questions in his eyes, the uncertainty beneath his power and bravado. "Gabe, what is it?"

His sweet smile poured across her senses like hot honey. "I've had sex with many women," he confessed, "but I've never in my life made love with someone who loved me back. You'll have to teach me how to do that."

She shivered, feeling her heart swell in her chest

like a butterfly unfolding its wings. "I never have either. We'll just have to play it by ear."

"An inspired suggestion," he replied huskily, and went on to show her why a woman's ear should be listed as a prime erogenous zone.

He drew her into his arms, into the white-hot glory of his love. Once again she was caught in the dark magic, the mystical binding that fused them together like two halves of a single sun. He eased her back on the bed, stripping her nightshirt from her body, leaving her all but naked beneath him. Then he lowered his head to her breast, and took her to paradise with a single flick of his tongue.

"You taste hot," he murmured as he continued to erotically suckle her breast. "Like chili peppers, Tabasco sauce, hot tamales."

She gave a breathless laugh. "You make me sound like one of *Tía Berta*'s meals."

"Better," he assured her, nipping exquisitely at her distended nipple. She gasped and arched beneath him, clutching the bed sheets for support. Laughter rumbled in his chest as he moved lower on her body. "Time for the next course."

His lips caressed her belly, moving closer to her hot, pulsing center. Desire tore through her like a savage beast, ripping her common sense to shreds. But with her last vestige of reason she recalled there was something she ought to tell him, something important. "Gabe, I'm a—"

Her words choked to silence as he kissed her through the sheer lace of her panties.

The world around her turned to sea froth, made of foam and air, fading away in the relentless tide of his loving. He rose from the bed and unzipped his jeans, the slow, rasping sound robbing her of whatever was left of her breath. He stripped off the rest of his restrictive clothing, standing beside her like a god from the sea, dark and powerful, magnificently male. Laurie's gaze riveted on his potent arousal. Moving wantonly, she gave a low, guttural, completely primitive moan.

"I'll take that as a compliment," he joked, though his voice betrayed his strain. He, too, was reaching the edge of his control. He stretched out on the bed, close but not touching her, and reached over to open the drawer to her bedside table.

Laurie stared in disbelief as he pulled out a small foil packet. "You put condoms in my nightstand?"

"I didn't want Adam to find them," he answered, as if that explained everything.

"But Gabe," she said, struggling to put her thoughts into words. "Bringing condoms. It's like . . . like you came to my apartment planning to seduce me."

"Of course I did," he said, looking at her like she was crazy to think otherwise.

She tried hard to be affronted, but that proved impossible. His answer was so arrogant, so honest, so uniquely Gabe that she found herself laughing instead. "Mister, you have a one-track mind when it comes to sex."

He covered her lips in a conquering kiss, drinking

in her laughter, feasting on her pleasure. "Sex I can get anytime. It's love I want from you, *puchunguita*." He stroked the textures of her mouth, even as his hands and body stroked the textures of her skin. "Tell me again," he breathed, his words tight and hot with longing. "Tell me again that you love me."

"I love you," she whispered in response. "I love you, I love you, I love you . . ." She repeated the words like a mantra, until she couldn't speak, couldn't think. Gabe's masterful hands caressed her into a frenzy, stripping away the last of her clothing and the last of her restraint. She writhed beneath him, her golden hair tangling with his sable, his darkness with her light. He whispered words of sin and promise in her ear, words she understood though the language he spoke them in was not her own.

Fear fell away from her like a discarded husk. TechniKon, the angels—they were nothing compared to his radiant power, the dark magic of his pirate's love. She gave herself up to his caresses, trusting him completely, opening herself to him with a joy so rich, she thought she'd die from the beauty of it. With a heart-stopping thrill she felt him probe her center, testing her readiness for the fullness of his love.

"*Dios*, you're tight," he said, his voice raw with need. He entered her just an inch, holding himself in check with iron control. "So damn tight. I'm not sure—"

"I am," she cried, not knowing if it was the truth, not caring. She spread herself wantonly, inviting him to take his pleasure, to claim her like his pirate ancestors had claimed their bounty, won by blood and fire. "I need you inside me. I need you, Gabe, *mi amor* . . ."

Her loving endearment pushed Gabe over the edge. Madness fired his blood. He thrust into her deeply, burying himself to the hilt in her hot, velvet sheath. But even that madness couldn't blind him to the brief spasm of pain on her face, or deafen him to the sound of her short, aborted cry. Cursing, he pulled himself out before fulfillment and reared back, watching in disbelief as new blood stained the sheets between her legs. The raging fire of his ecstasy was doused by the cold water of reality. He fell heavily beside her, exhausted, astonished, and confused as hell.

"Válgame Dios, you're a virgin!"

ELEVEN

For a long time he just held her, cradling her against him, murmuring endearments that he knew could never make up for what had happened between them. She cried a little, her silent tears slipping down her cheeks like bitter rain. One of her tears dripped onto his chest, cool against his still-hot skin, making him wince with a particular kind of pain. He felt as if he'd destroyed something fragile and priceless, and there was no way on earth he could put it back together again.

Gradually he felt her begin to relax, her tension ease. Unfortunately, that did nothing to soothe the tightness in his own muscles, the pain that constricted his heart. He'd never in his life hurt a woman—now he'd managed to wound the one he loved the most.

"Are you all right?" he asked finally.

She nodded, but didn't look up at him. "I'm sorry," she confessed to the crook in his arm. "I should have told you, but I didn't want to spoil . . . well, I thought I could keep it from you. Some men don't notice."

"Some men are pigs," he said harshly. He laid his forehead against her shoulder and gave a long, ragged sigh. "Dammit, Laurie, I hurt you."

"No," she cried softly. She turned in his arms and took his face between her hands, pressing fragile, candy-sweet kisses on his cheeks and the corners of his mouth. "You could never hurt me. Never. I love you."

She still loves me. He breathed a silent prayer, knowing a part of him would have died if he'd lost her love. Relief and gratitude coursed through him, along with other emotions, less commendable.

He'd never been with a virgin, but he knew damn well she'd need some time to heal before she made love again. Unfortunately, his body had other ideas. The brief moments he'd shared her body had taken him closer to heaven than he'd ever been, and there was a base, raging part of his nature that was so crazy to get back inside her, it didn't care whether she was ready for him or not. Even now he grew hard, remembering the incredible heat of her, the way they'd fit as if they'd been made for each other, the impossible rightness . . .

Self-consciously he moved to the other side of the bed, using a well-placed pillow to hide the evidence of his inconvenient desire. The distance helped—until he looked back. During their lovemaking the moon had risen, shining into the room through a slit in the curtains. Laurie lay in a pool of moonlight, her porcelain body clothed only in a tangle of gossamer-fine hair. His breath rushed out in a strangled gasp. *Dios,* how was a man supposed to resist this kind of temptation?

"I know what you're thinking," she said quietly.

Gabe doubted it. If she had any inkling of the graphically sexual images consuming his mind, she'd have thrown him out on his ear.

She drew herself up on her elbow and continued. "You're wondering about my son."

"Adam," he mused. He'd been so concerned with Laurie that he'd forgotten about the boy sleeping peacefully in the next room, the boy he realized now could not possibly be her child. "Who is he?"

"He's my son."

Gabe plowed his hands through his sweat-matted hair, wondering why fate had chosen him to fall in love with such a stubborn, caring woman. "Laurie, I know you love Adam *like* he was your own flesh and blood, but I think we've just proved—"

"You don't understand," she interrupted. She sat up and moved closer to him, her eyes wide with haunting vulnerability. "I've wanted to tell you so many times," she said, her voice barely above a whisper, "but I knew you wouldn't believe me. I almost don't believe it myself sometimes. Until I remember about the angels . . ."

"Stop it, *cara,*" Gabe ordered, frightened by the vagueness in her tone. He reached out and took her by the shoulders, giving her a gentle but decisive squeeze. "The angels are a bad dream. But I'm real. My love for you is real."

He paused, and smiled a grin that somehow managed to be devilish and endearing at once. "If I moved this damn pillow out of the way, you'd see just how *real* it is."

Her throaty laugh dipped his heavy heart in gold. "I do love you, Gabe. And because I love you I want you to know the truth, so you'll understand why I can't . . ." Her words dwindled off as fresh tears glittered in her eyes. "Damn, I wish I could stop crying."

To hell with this, Gabe thought. He started to pull her close, but she twisted out of his grasp like quicksilver. She moved to the other side of the bed and drew the sheets up to cover her breasts, as if she were suddenly afraid of his gaze. "Promise me you won't talk or touch me until I finish. I won't have the courage to tell you if you do." Then she pushed back her heavy curtain of hair and smiled at him—the sad, bittersweet smile of a fallen angel—and began to tell him her story.

"My mother didn't have time for a child in her social life. Later, she didn't want me around to remind her progressively younger boyfriends of her real age. I spent my school years being shuttled between boarding schools, getting the best education money could buy. Luckily, I was bright enough to take advantage of it. I skipped several grades, graduating high school when I was sixteen, and college when I was nineteen. By twenty-three I'd already completed my medical training and was building a reputation in the field of genetic engineering. That was when TechniKon approached me and made me an offer I couldn't refuse."

Her smile tightened, growing harsher with self-condemning memories. "Looking back, I realize I should have asked more questions, done more research on the company before I agreed to join them. But it seemed like an answer to a dream. TechniKon presented itself as being a big, happy family. I'd never had a family, you see."

She looked down and absently creased the edge of the sheet. "They put me in charge of one of their genetic research teams. It was heady stuff for a twenty-three-year-old—the newest high-tech equipment and a dozen lab assistants at her command. It's no excuse, but I really didn't think about the consequences of the experiment I'd been assigned until it was too late."

"What kind of experiment?" Gabe asked, an awful suspicion forming in his mind.

"To tear a page from the book of life. To take DNA sequences and clone them together into a living organism." She paused, her voice heavy with quiet dread as she added, "A *human* organism."

Suddenly, the puzzle pieces of her life came rushing together in Gabe's mind. The running, the fear, the existence of a son who could not possibly be her son. . . .

"Adam," he said, dropping the name like a stone in the silence. "Mother of God, you cloned Adam."

"Yes," she replied softly, feeling again the enormity of what she'd done. She'd been so starry-eyed over TechniKon's praises that she hadn't questioned, hadn't thought . . . until she'd looked into the microscope and seen Adam's tiny heart beating steady and strong. Something had happened to her own heart at that moment, something wonderful and sacred, and completely unscientific. In a pristine lab, under the eyes of a half-dozen somber, unsuspecting assistants, she silently celebrated the birth of her son.

"We were forbidden to discuss our work with anyone outside the company," she continued. "Much of TechniKon's funding comes from conservative political groups who'd be appalled to know they'd been experimenting in procreation. I suppose I should have wondered what would happen after we took Adam out of the artificial womb, but I was too worried about keeping him alive. No one had ever done anything like this before, and he was so little, so terribly fragile. Toward the end I brought a cot into the lab and slept beside the incubation unit, just to make sure I'd be near him if anything happened. The happiest day of my life was when I broke the unit's seal, and I held my little boy in my arms."

She stole a look at Gabe, but the moon had risen past her window, casting the room once more into murky darkness. She could barely make out his shadowed figure, much less his expression. What was he thinking? she wondered. Too easily, her troubled mind supplied an answer.

He despised her for playing God, for putting the

advancement of science before the sanctity of life. Like Eve, she'd picked the apple from the tree of knowledge. Only in her case, the apple was a blameless little boy.

"What happened then?" Gabe asked, his low tone giving away nothing of his private feelings.

"I hadn't given much thought to Adam's future, but TechniKon had. The directors learned that they could make a tidy profit from selling my research—as long as Adam was included in the deal." She closed her eyes, wincing at the memory of her naive foolishness. "They considered my son to be a piece of laboratory property, like a Bunsen burner, or a test tube.

"I couldn't let that happen. I smuggled Adam out of the lab and hid him with a friend, then went back for my research. That's when the angels caught me. They locked me up, and tried to make me tell—" Her words were cut short by the sudden grip of a hand around her wrist.

"Did they harm you?"

He has the eyes of a cat, she thought, distracted by his nearness. His fingers circled her arm with comforting strength, reassuring her more than words ever could. She breathed deep, taking his musky, masculine scent into her lungs. For the moment it didn't matter whether he still cared for her or not. It only mattered that he was here.

"Did they harm you?" he repeated, his voice edged with anger.

"Only with words. To them I was a meek, mild-mannered scientist—I don't think they expected me to put up much of a fight." Laurie's mouth pulled into a wry grin at the memory. "They *definitely* didn't expect me to brain my guard with a folding chair and escape with the bulk of my research."

Gabe's grip on her wrist tightened possessively. "It's a good thing they didn't touch you," he commented with deceptive calm. "Otherwise, I would have had to cut the heart out of every one of them."

She believed him. Gabe, her own personal pirate, had pledged to protect her and Adam, and he was not a man to go back on his promises. Still, his words spoke of obligation, not love. "Gabe, I need to know. After what I've told you about myself, do you still . . . can you still . . . ?"

"*Dios, puchunguita*, as if you have to ask."

He pulled her roughly into his arms, enfolding her in a tremendous bear hug that all but squeezed the breath from her body. She didn't care. Loving Gabe, and knowing he loved her, was the bright and burning center of her existence. Breathing was optional.

He whispered cherishing words against her hair. She was so overwhelmed by love and relief that she didn't hear him at first, but gradually his words sank in, bringing with them a new wave of love, and dread.

". . . can go to the press," he was saying. "You can use your research as evidence. And when we tell them about Adam—"

"But we can't," she said despairingly. "I burned the research, to keep TechniKon from getting it back even if they caught us. Besides, I can't tell *anyone* about Adam. If word got out, he'd be labeled a freak. His life would be ruined, just as surely as if I'd handed him over to TechniKon. However he came into this world, he's just a boy—a smart, but otherwise very ordinary little boy. I want him to have a normal life."

"So you drag him from city to city," Gabe said bluntly.

"It's a better life than growing up as a carnival attraction," she said with equal candor. She curled up against his chest, wanting him to understand how much giving Adam a normal life meant to her, but not knowing how to do it.

"You don't know what it's like to be alone, Gabe, not really. Even when you lost your parents you were surrounded by a loving family. But I grew up virtually alone in the world, too shy to make friends, and too smart to pretend it didn't matter. Adam's situation would be ten times worse, a hundred times worse. I couldn't bear it—"

"Hush," Gabe said as he lowered his face to kiss away her tears. His mouth brushed her lips with exquisite reverence, a wordless prayer of compassion. "We'll talk about Adam in the morning. Tonight, this moment, is for us."

He scattered kisses across her cheeks and throat, tiny sparks that kindled a raging forest fire inside her. The sheet covering her body dropped with a sigh, leaving no secrets between them, no ancient wounds to tarnish their passion. Gabe's mouth plundered hers with a new intimacy, a special and profound sharing that had as much to do with her giving as with his taking. He stroked her breasts and thighs, every touch bringing her to a higher level of awareness, a deeper understanding of their love. She ached for the completion of that love, but reality intervened, reminding her of their first disastrous attempt at lovemaking. "Gabe, I want to, but I can't—"

"I know," he replied, his voice smooth as silk against her skin. "But there are other ways, other things we can do. Let me give you this, *puchunguita*. Let me show you how it was meant to be between a man and a woman. . . ."

In the heat and the darkness he loved her unselfishly, stroking and caressing her until she cried out in sweet fulfillment. Still holding her, he waited until her passion passed, and her breathing slowed into the rich, peaceful cadence of dreamless sleep.

He, however, remained wide awake. He stared into the shadows above her bed, going over and over the things she'd told him, seeking a solution. In his career as a private investigator Gabe had unraveled many mysteries, some considered unsolvable. But he'd never dealt with a problem with so much at stake, or one dearer to his heart. Laurie couldn't sacrifice her son's happiness—Gabe wouldn't want her to. Yet the thought of not having Laurie in his life was equally unacceptable. Quandaries and questions blew through his mind like his ancestors' dreaded nor'easters. *¡Concho!* this was a mess.

Dawn was just beginning to creep through the bedroom curtains when he hit upon a kind of solution. He got up, taking care not to wake her, then scooped his jeans off the floor beside the bed. He pulled them on and headed for the door, pausing just once to take a final look at the woman he loved. Her hair fell across the pillow like a golden shower, and her body was still curved to the shape of him. As he watched she reached out to the now-empty place where he'd laid, murmuring his name in her sleep.

That was all he could take. He left the bedroom and silently collected his belongings, slipping out of the apartment before he had a chance to change his mind. There were things he had to do, things he couldn't take care of with Laurie at his side. Besides, she might not agree with his plans. Hell, he could practically guarantee she wouldn't, but it might be their only chance to stay together.

TWELVE

"Laurie? *Chiquita*, are you all right?"

The sound of Uncle Carlos's concerned voice shook Laurie out of her private thoughts. She placed the last of the guava fruits she'd been stacking on the top of the meticulously arranged pile. "I'm fine," she answered brightly. "Why do you ask?"

Carlos stroked his chin. "Oh, no reason. Except that you've just stacked a dozen guavas on Berta's grapefruit display."

Startled, Laurie glanced at the fruit in front of her. Carlos was absolutely right. She'd stacked the small, brown guavas on top of the large yellow grapefruits, never noticing the difference. *Hell*, she thought as she began to retrieve the guavas. This was her last full week working at *Tía Berta's* store. She wanted to do her best. But her mind kept wandering to an event that took place almost two weeks ago.

Twelve days, thirteen hours, and twenty-six minutes to be exact. . . .

Carlos cleared his throat, recapturing her attention. "Something tells me you have more on your mind than grapefruit and guavas," he said in a voice that wrapped like a warm blanket around her troubled heart. "Something that begins with the same letter, perhaps, but has less of an IQ?"

Laurie fought a grin at the man's unflattering description of his nephew. *Gabe isn't the only one I'm going to miss,* she thought as another little arrow of sadness buried itself in her heart. "*Tio,* why is it you can always make me smile?"

"Because I care about you," Carlos answered. Then, giving her a quick wink, he added, "And I know a certain guava-brained young man who does too."

Laurie's tenuous smile died. Carlos hadn't meant to, but he'd inadvertently touched a raw nerve. Twelve days, thirteen hours, and twenty-six minutes ago she had felt she'd known Gabe's heart better than her own. His tender loving had made her believe all over again in rainbows and promises and tomorrows, but she'd woken up alone.

He'd left her a scribbled note, saying that he had to go out of town on business. No explanation, no length of time, no destination. Very infuriating. Exasperated, she'd been half tempted to crumple the note into a ball and toss it into the nearest wastebasket. She would have, except for one thing. Scrawled near the bottom of the paper was the half-illegible word "love." That single word made the note the most precious thing she owned.

Since that morning she hadn't heard anything from Gabe. She'd called Yoli immediately, but the older woman was almost as much in the dark as she was. Gabe had left his secretary a similar abbreviated message, only adding that he'd appreciate it if she and Carlos would keep an eye out for Laurie while he was gone. "Don't worry, dear," Yoli had assured her in a voice seasoned by long-suffering patience, "he does this all the time. Never thinks to tell anyone where he's going, or how long he'll be. But I know he's absolutely fine. I read his horoscope this morning, and it said his planets were aligned in an extremely fortunate aspect. . . ."

Laurie doubted the same could be said of her own horoscope.

Fulfilling Gabe's request, either Carlos or Yoli had spoken to her every day, sometimes taking her and Adam to lunch, or treating Adam to a movie or a Marlins' baseball game. Laurie appreciated their kindness, but it did little to fill the emptiness in her heart. The days without Gabe slipped away like gems dropped in deep water, priceless treasures never to be retrieved. And they had so little time left to begin with.

Oh, good grief, she thought sternly, *I'm beginning to sound like a bad greeting card.* She'd never let herself indulge in self-pity, and by heaven she wasn't going to start now. Resolutely, she pulled the hem of her heavy burlap produce apron up to form a basket, and began retrieving the misstacked guavas. "Thanks for stopping by, Carlos. Let me know if you hear anything about when Gabe's coming back."

"But my dear," Carlos said, a puzzled expression crossing his brow, "Gabe *is* back."

Laurie almost lost her grip on her apron. "Back? In Little Havana?"

The older man nodded. "Yoli told me he called late yesterday, and said he was on his way home. Forgive me, but I assumed he'd already spoken to you."

Laurie would have assumed the same thing. If Gabe had returned, there was no reason why he wouldn't have called her either last night, or this morning. Unless he hadn't returned after all. Unless he'd been delayed, either by the job he was working on, or something else, or *someone* else. . . .

Frightening images poured into her mind like water through a breached dam. In this insular Latin community Gabe was king, but outside he was just another man, unprotected by his friends and family, alone. Had he said something, or done something, to put TechniKon on his trail?

The logical portion of Laurie's mind dismissed the idea as ridiculous. The angels hadn't tracked her down yet, much less linked Gabe to her. But the emotional side of her grew more anxious by the second. She knew firsthand just how vindictive TechniKon could be. If anything happened to Gabe because of her, she'd never—

"I'm sure he's fine, my dear," Uncle Carlos said, answering her unspoken thoughts.

"How did you—?"

"I'm no mind reader," he said, smiling at her concern. "But your beautiful eyes—they show your feelings clearer than any words." Still smiling, he reached over to the grapefruit stack and picked up a couple of guavas. "Now, let's get these little troublemakers back where they belong. . . ."

Carlos helped her restack the errant produce, entertaining her with a series of jokes and stories that made her laugh for the first time in a week. But when he left the grocery store, her bright spirits left with him.

Worry closed around her like a storm cloud, worry for Gabe and what might have happened to him. She stood at the counter, trying to focus her mind on nursing the old cash register through one more afternoon of customers. But every time she rang up a purchase, she heard her lover's name echoed in her mind. Gabe, Gabe. *Where in the hell was he?*

"Hi, Laurie."

She looked over the top of the register and saw Tony, the boy she'd helped through the Man O' War sting, smiling up at her. "Well, hi. How's your side?"

"Great," the boy answered. "I'm almost back to normal. This morning Gabe told me that I could crew again in a couple of—"

"Gabe?" she cried, latching on to the name. "You saw Gabe this morning?"

"Of course. All of us did."

"All?" Laurie questioned, confusion mixing with relief.

Her thoughts were interrupted by another young voice, equally familiar.

"Got any sodas?" Jimmy asked as he approached the counter. "Gabe said he'd spot me a soda. How you doing, Laurie?"

Not as well as a minute ago, she thought, totally confused. "Let me get this straight. You boys have seen Gabe today?"

"Course we have," Jimmy answered. "We spent the morning on *Dulcinea*, cleaning her up. I polished the brass."

"I swabbed the deck," Tony offered.

I worried my brains out, Laurie added silently, recalling what she'd done this morning.

Another voice interrupted her thoughts—deep and resonate and, until a few moments ago, well loved.

"Good afternoon, *puchunguita*," Gabe said as he entered Berta's grocery store, carrying a huge bouquet of red roses. Smiling with the wattage of a thousand suns, he strode up to the counter and offered the flowers to Laurie.

She made no move to take the bouquet. He'd been gone for twelve days, thirteen—no fourteen—hours, twenty-six minutes . . . and he spent the morning polishing the brass on *Dulcinea!* Fuming, she looked at Gabe, then at the flowers, then back at Gabe again. "Why waste them on me? Give them to your bloody boat!"

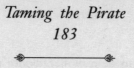
"I guess she doesn't like roses," Jimmy said.

"I guess not," Tony agreed as he watched Laurie stalk away. "Some people are allergic to roses. Do you think she's allergic, Gabe?"

"Not to roses," Gabe commented, using his free hand to rub his pounding forehead. Damn! he'd had nothing but headaches for a week and a half. He'd spent lonely nights on the road, eaten food from soon-to-be-condemned diners, argued for three days solid with a fellow private investigator until he finally agreed to take on some of his cases—all to get back to his woman as soon as he could. Now it looked as if that woman had gone certifiably loco while he was away.

Dios, things like this weren't supposed to happen to a pirate!

Still holding the rejected bouquet, he followed her down the narrow aisle toward the back of the store. "Laurie, what's wrong?"

"Wrong?" Laurie said, sidestepping to avoid Mrs. Mendoza's overloaded cart. "What could be wrong? You're away for a week and a half, and you spend the morning . . . playing Blackbeard!"

"Blackbeard was English," Gabe replied as he gingerly navigated his arms, legs, and roses around the portly Mrs. Mendoza. "And I wasn't *playing* at anything. I was cleaning up *Dulcinea*. She was in pretty bad shape."

"Right. Lord help us if *Dulcinea* gets a speck of dust on her. Laurie, however, can go to—"

She never finished. Whipping around to face him, her heavy apron caught on the bottom tier of a stack of canned mushrooms. The stack collapsed, sending dozens of cans rolling across the aisle.

"Damn," she said, dropping to her knees beside the mess.

He saw her reach out and try to collect a can, but her nervous fingers clutched too early, and the contrary can rolled farther away. Apparently this was the last straw for Laurie. She sat back on her heels, covering her face with her hands.

"Just leave me alone. I'll be fine in a while."

Leaving was the last thing Gabe intended to do. He set the flowers on a nearby shelf and hunkered down in front of her, studying her with concern. For all her brave anger she was shaking, caught up in the tumultuous emotions inside her. Laurie was too rational to get this upset over a "bloody boat." There was more to her anger than that.

He didn't know what was wrong, but he had a suspicion—one that left him as cold inside as her anger was hot. "Laurie," he asked slowly, "is this about the other night? I mean, have your feelings for me . . . changed?"

Her hands fell to her lap. She stared at him, her indigo eyes wide with surprise, and shining with the gentle love that warmed him in ways the sun never could. She leaned forward and shaped her hand to the curve of his cheek. "Honestly, Gabe," she said as her mouth pulled into a reluctant smile, "I've worked with chemical compounds smarter than you are. Nothing could change the way I feel about you. Nothing."

Gabe let out an undisguised sigh of relief. "Then why are you so angry?"

"Because—" she began, then stopped as emotion overcame her. She pulled back her hand, and balled it with her other one into a tight fist in her lap. "Because you're gone for over a week, and I was worried sick about you. Then, when you come back, you don't even bother to call. Instead, you spend the day on *Dulcinea* without me. And we've got so little time left . . ."

She didn't know. *Concho*, how could she since he hadn't told her yet! He shook his head, cursing himself as the world's worst fool. "It's all right, *cara*. I've—"

He stopped as he caught sight of the sizable Mrs. Mendoza, owl eyed and attentive, listening eagerly to every word. Glancing around, Gabe saw that other customers had also gathered near them, some apparently fascinated with the labels on nearby canned goods, while other, more honest patrons were just openly eavesdropping. This was *not* the place to hold a private conversation.

He stood and held down his hand for Laurie. "We're getting out of here."

She nodded, but didn't take his hand. "Just let me get these cans restacked. Then I'll close out the register, and check with *Tía* to see if there's anything else she needs."

"*Tía*'s chores can wait." He bent down and grasped Laurie around the waist, pulling her to her feet as if she weighed no more than a rag doll. "I'm tired of waiting. We're going. Now."

Laurie gave a huff of righteous indignation. "Right. *You* make me wait all morning, then *you* waltz in here and expect me to drop everything—hey!"

Her words stopped abruptly as he picked her up and slung her over his shoulder. "You talk too much," he commented as he retrieved the roses and started down the aisle.

"Gabe, put me down. This is kidnapping!"

He grinned, thinking his pirate ancestors would approve. Apparently the customers did as well, for as he walked down the aisle they greeted him with laughter and intermittent applause. He passed the counter, and caught sight of Laurie's son standing next to Jimmy, laughing with the rest of them.

"Adam!" Laurie exclaimed, clearly annoyed by her son's defection.

Gabe chuckled. "Don't blame him too much, *puchunguita*. I asked the boys to include him in their afternoon softball game. Quite an honor for a boy his age. And I've arranged for Yoli to take care of him tonight."

"Tonight?" she said. "Who said anything about tonight?"

Gabe's smile deepened. "I did. I'm going to take

you for a ride on that 'bloody boat,' *cara*. And we're going to have a long talk. Eventually."

It did turn out to be a long time before they talked, but not for the reasons Gabe anticipated. Extra vacation traffic in the marina made it an obstacle course, as amateur captains and inexperienced crews blithely steered their crafts toward certain disaster. It took all of Gabe's piloting skills to get *Dulcinea* safely to the harbor mouth.

More than once Laurie heard him mutter a curse in guttural Spanish, and although she didn't recognize the words she understood their meaning loud and clear. In fact, after a few near misses with clueless commanders, she found herself wishing for a deck-mounted cannon or two herself.

Once they made open water, however, their troubles disappeared like sea foam into sand. Laurie sat with her feet dangling over the bow, and her chin resting on the railing, relishing the feel of the sleek, powerful ship beneath her. Under Gabe's skilled hands *Dulcinea* cut through the waves with the eagerness of a diving dolphin, heading for deep water and the empty, endless horizon. Laurie drank in deep breaths of the brisk salt wind, glorying in the freedom of the boundless expanse of sky and water. She pretended for a moment that her future was just as unlimited. She pretended, for a moment, that she had a future.

"A gold doubloon for your thoughts," Gabe said behind her.

Laurie turned and watched him walk toward her, his footing sure and stable on the rolling deck of his craft. He seemed to know instinctively every shift *Dulcinea* was about to make, anticipating her every movement. The sea's in his blood, Laurie thought, admiring the confidence of his steps, the catlike grace of his body. If only the uncertainties they faced on dry land were this predictable. "Who's steering the boat?"

He laughed, a sound as free as the wind. He grasped the bow railing and swung down beside her. "Pirate victims aren't supposed to ask questions like that."

She couldn't resist a smile. "Sorry. I didn't know there was a code of conduct I had to follow."

"Certainly. You're supposed to kick and scream for a while. Then you fall into my arms in a passionate embrace." He smiled an endearingly devilish grin that melted her heart like butter. "We can skip right to the last part, though."

Lord, she loved this man. He could drive her crazy faster than anyone on earth, but his intrinsic decency, his sincerity—and his contagious sense of humor—bound her to him more securely than any pirate chains. He was as gloriously generous and wickedly unpredictable as the sea beneath them, and she wished she could spend her life learning the tides of his nature. But that wish, like so many others, was far beyond her reach.

She looked out at the distant horizon, thinking how vast it was, and how wide the world was beyond it. Two people didn't mean much in the grand scheme of things, even two people very much in love. Suddenly she felt very small and helpless, and terribly alone. Still gazing at the horizon she murmured sadly, "Maybe this wasn't such a good idea after all."

She felt his strong, warm fingers cover her own. He bent close to her, and whispered in her ear. "Do you trust me?"

His breath, hot against her skin, kindled the ashes of fires she was desperately trying to stamp out. "It's not a question of trust," she told him honestly. "It's a question of reality. No matter how much we love each other, we can't be together. Some things aren't meant to be."

Every word had cost her blood, but as she turned to look at him she saw that they apparently hadn't affected Gabe in the least. He still wore the same devilish grin, and his eyes still sparkled with maddening mischief.

"So you think we're not meant to be?" he said, giving her hand a reassuring squeeze. "Well, let me tell you the story of my great-great-, etc. grandfather Rodrigo, a ship's captain—"

"Pirate ship?" Laurie asked.

"Of course." He lifted his hand from hers and circled her shoulders, pulling her gently against him in a companionable embrace. "Now listen to the story. One day while great-grandfather Rodrigo was pacing the bridge he passed a ship—"

"A pirate ship?"

"*Concho*, you ask more questions than Adam," he said, giving her shoulders a shake. "I don't know if it was a pirate ship. It doesn't matter."

"Well, it might not matter to you, but it probably mattered a lot to your great-grandfa—"

Gabe clamped his free hand over her mouth, effectively silencing her. "As I was saying *before I was interrupted*, Rodrigo's ship passed another one going in the opposite direction. The channel was narrow at that point, so they came within yards of each other. And on the deck of the other ship my great-grandfather saw the most beautiful woman in the world."

Laurie's laugh was muffled by Gabe's hand.

"All right, so it's unbelievable. But I tell you my great-grandfather was so smitten by the unknown beauty that he turned his ship around and sailed after her. A storm came up, and Rodrigo had his hands full keeping his ship from capsizing. When the storm cleared, the other ship was nowhere to be seen."

"Uch fe oh hen?" Laurie asked.

Glancing a warning, Gabe removed his hand.

"I said, what did he do then?"

"He went from port to port, searching for the beautiful woman. Some say he searched for months, some say for years." He lifted his chin and stared out toward the distant horizon, as if he, too, were searching for his ancestor's lost love. "It doesn't matter how long he searched, though, because in the end he found her. They married and lived happily ever after."

Laurie tilted up her head to see his face. The sun had just begun to set, lacing his ebony hair with ruddy fire. His classically handsome features could have belonged to a Spanish man of any century, from one of Cortez's conquistadors to the determined Rodrigo himself. For a moment she imagined she was the nameless woman on the ship, and Gabe the tenacious Rodrigo. "That is the most beautiful story I've ever heard," she said, burrowing closer to his chest. "And I don't believe a word of it."

Gabe threw back his head and laughed heartily. "All right, so I changed it a little. Rodrigo didn't see a woman on the deck of the other ship, he saw a man who owed him money. But he still tracked him down, proving that Ramirez men don't give up the things they want." Looking down, his eyes captured hers with a gaze so intense, it knocked the breath from her lungs. "I think you know what I'm trying to say, *puchunguita.*"

"Gabe," she whispered hoarsely, "it won't work. I love you, but I can't put Adam at risk by staying."

"I agree," he said.

"You . . . agree?"

"Of course," he said, tucking a strand of her hair tenderly behind her ear. "You are absolutely right. If you stay here, TechniKon will eventually find you and Adam. You can't stay, and I don't intend to lose you." He smiled, the last of the sunlight glinting off his teeth as he added, "That is why I am going with you."

THIRTEEN

He loved it when she got angry. She became so charmingly flustered, like a cockatiel fluffing its feathers for battle. *My little golden bird*, he thought, grinning at her less than deadly ire. He'd known she wouldn't accept his idea at first, but he intended to spend the rest of the day convincing her. And the rest of the night, if that was what it took. In fact, he looked forward to it.

"Gabe, you can't go with me!"

"Oh, but I can, *cara*," he assured her. Under her thin veneer of toughness she was heartbreakingly innocent, and fragile as blown glass. It was a miracle she and her son had survived on their own this long. "It's all arranged. I've finished up most of my outstanding cases, and handed the rest off to other private investigators. I've talked to Carlos about my legal affairs, and how to arrange for our new identities—"

"You've talked to Carlos," she said, her eyes widening in alarm. "Carlos *knows?*"

"Don't worry. *Tío Carlos* rivals the grave in keeping secrets. He won't tell. He—" Gabe paused, his attention suddenly demanded by the sights and sounds of the sea around him. He lifted his head, sniffing the wind for smells he couldn't name, listening for watery whispers too subtle to be captured in words. Senses bred into him long before his birth informed him that they had reached their destination, the northern edge of the coral reef. A split second later the bell on his navigation computer went off, unnecessarily confirming his suspicions.

"Forgive me, *puchunguita*," he said as he reluctantly let her go and pulled himself to his feet. "I've got to drop anchor or we'll drift to Freeport. But I'll be back. We've got a lot to discuss. . . ."

Moments later he maneuvered across the gunnel to the aft of the boat, deftly using ropes and railings to keep his balance. Like the sea she rode on, *Dulcinea* could be fickle at times. It was never wise to take her for granted. Reaching the control console, he cut the small motor which had been keeping them on course while he talked with Laurie. Then he dropped the anchor, and waited for the telltale tug that would indicate it had caught on the reef below.

"Gabe."

He turned, and saw that Laurie had followed him from the bow. He'd been so absorbed in his thoughts that he hadn't heard her approach, even though she now stood just a few feet away from him. The sunset spilled over her, staining her white cotton dress and pale hair with the color of blood. A cold tinge of foreboding crept up his spine. *Concho*, he thought as he shrugged off the feeling, *Yoli and her damn cards must be getting to me. . . .*

"Gabe, you are not going with me, and that's final," she stated, crossing her arms determinedly in front of her. "It's very decent and upstanding of you to offer, but—"

"Decent and upstanding?" he repeated, appalled by her choice of words. "You make me sound like one of those statues in the park." He sat down on the side of the boat, and crossed his arms just as determinedly. "I'm not made of stone, *puchunguita. You* of all people should know that."

He heard her hushed gasp, and knew she was remembering the glory of their night together. He recalled it, too, and felt his blood heat in response, quick and demanding. Driven by need, he reached out for her but she stiffened, and skittered beyond his grasp. *Dios*, she was more trouble to land than a marlin!

"I can't let . . ." She paused, swallowing hard before continuing. "I can't let you make this kind of sacrifice. Your life and family are here in Miami. You'd be giving up everything to be with me and Adam."

"Not everything," he growled.

She lifted her chin, and gave him a stern look that probably would have worked wonders on quieting a roomful of note-taking geneticists. Unfortunately, it made Gabe want to laugh.

"You are not thinking sensibly about this. You've got family and friends here that you care about, and who care about you. When you think about it logically, I know—" She stopped, her stern mask faltering as she struggled to speak the next words. "I know you will see that I'm right."

Gabe watched her closely. Emotions flitted across her face, subtle to some, but achingly apparent to him. She loved him fiercely—but that love had more chance of driving her away than binding her to him. Once again she reminded him of a marlin dancing on the line, fighting against the inevitable. But even strong lines could break under extreme pressure. He knew that if this little fish got away, he hadn't a hope in hell of hooking her again. . . .

"Okay," he said.

"Okay what?"

"Okay, you're right," he answered, shrugging. "I've thought about it, logically. I've got too good a life here to give it all up for you." He got up and brushed past her as he started toward the bow of the boat. "You're not worth it."

She didn't answer. For a long, uncertain moment he wondered if he'd misjudged her, and the strength of her love for him. Then he heard a scrape and a shuffle behind him.

"Hey, wait just a minute," she cried.

Gabe let out the breath he didn't know he was holding. He glanced back and saw that she was storm-

ing after him, just as he'd hoped she would. Smother-
ing a grin, he leaned nonchalantly against the bow
railing. "You want something, *puchunguita?*"

"I want to know what you're up to." She stepped
carefully across *Dulcinea*'s slightly rolling deck, her
movements less graceful than Gabe's, but just as decisive. She stopped in front of him, planting her feet
apart for extra balance. "Why did you agree so
quickly?"

"You made sense," Gabe said, turning his head to
look out at the water. "Hmm, the sea's getting
rougher, but I don't think it's anything to worry a—"

"Gabe, stop it!"

He swung back to face her, his expression as innocent as a newborn babe's. "Stop what?"

"You know very well what!" she stated, placing
her hands on her hips. "You're pretending it doesn't
matter, like you don't care if I leave without you. But
you do care. That's why you're pretending you
don't."

Gabe folded his arms over his chest, and cocked
an eyebrow in amusement. "Interesting theory,
puchunguita. You pick that up on *Donahue?*"

"Honestly, you can be so *infuriating!*" She balled
her fist and shook it at him. "You aren't taking me
seriously."

Quick as a cat his hand lashed out and closed
around her wrist, pulling her to him. "I take you *very*
seriously," he said with lethal softness. "But make no
mistake. You belong to me. I've claimed your body,
and—though you try to deny it—your heart. You are

mine, *cara*. And if you think you're getting away from me on this side of the grave, think again."

Her mouth hovered a breath away from his. He wanted like hell to kiss her, to taste the sweet fire that burned only for him, but he held himself back. Taking her now would simply prove that she wanted him, not that she trusted him. He had to let her make the first move. But Dios, he thought as the ache of desire ripped through his middle, she'd better make it soon.

She didn't make that move, but neither did he. A sudden swell caught *Dulcinea* broadside, tilting her unexpectedly. Gabe felt the shift and pushed Laurie away from the edge of the boat to safety. But in doing so he lost his own balance, and toppled backward over the bow railing, into the sea.

"Gabe!" Laurie cried as she rushed to the railing. She scanned the dark waters, searching frantically for some sign of where he'd fallen. She felt as if her heart had stopped beating. *If I don't see him in the next few seconds I'm going in, whether I can swim or—*

He surfaced with the force of a rising dolphin, sending crystal drops flying. Looking up, he smoothed back his drenched hair and uttered a raw Cuban curse.

Raw or not, it was music to Laurie's ears. "Gabe, are you all right?"

"I'm fine," he called back, "except the women in my life are trying to murder me. Whose idea was this —yours or *Dulcinea*'s?"

"Gabe," Laurie said, laughing with relief. "Oh Gabe, I thought you'd drowned."

"Well, I still might if I don't get out of here. My jeans weigh a ton. I need your help, *cara.*"

"Anything," she promised.

He swam up to the side of the boat beneath her, his strokes smooth and effortless despite the weight of his drenched clothing. "I need you to let down *Dulcinea*'s back platform." Then, giving her a devilish wink, he added, "For starters."

In less than a minute she'd unhooked the platform, and watched it splash to the surface. Gabe grasped the edge and hauled himself up with the ease of a practiced gymnast. He's safe, she thought with grateful relief.

That relief changed rapidly to another emotion as she watched him pull his sopping shirt over his head and deposit it on the platform beside him.

"What . . . what are you doing?" she asked, struggling not to stare at his naked torso.

"I'm not getting back on *Dulcinea* like this," he stated, indicating his drenched blue jeans. "The boys and I spent the whole day cleaning her. No way am I going to mess her up."

"Are you going to take off . . . everything?"

"Only what's wet," he assured her.

Oh God, she thought as she visualized Gabe walking around on *Dulcinea*, naked as the day he was born. She'd been able to keep a rein on her feelings up to this point, but faced with that kind of temptation . . .

She swallowed, finding that her mouth had suddenly gone bone-dry. "This isn't going to change things. I'm not going to change my mind."

His only answer was a smile.

She turned away, anger building inside her like a thunderhead. The man was insufferable! He thought that by just "strutting his stuff" he would make her forget all about her resolutions and cave in to his will. The fact that he was probably right only added to her frustration.

"Dammit," she muttered, "doesn't he understand I'm doing this for him?" Leaning heavily on *Dulcinea*'s railing, she looked out across the western skyline, and the bannered glory of the dying day. *Part of you is dying too,* her mind whispered.

She shrugged off the thought, refusing to get sucked into the useless quagmire of self-pity. Yes, leaving Gabe was going to be the hardest thing she'd ever done in her life. Just a few days away from him had shown her how vital he was to her, how his laughter and love, even his bad-boy arrogance, scattered life-giving water across the barren landscape of her soul. She doubted she'd ever find a way to fill the emptiness inside her. But she couldn't ask him to sacrifice his entire life for her.

Gabe had a secure home and a loving family, the two greatest treasures in the world as far as Laurie was concerned. She knew their importance even if Gabe didn't. She wasn't going to let him give them up just for her. He deserved better than a life on the run with a hunted fugitive. Even if this particular fugitive loved him with every fiber of her being. . . .

"Laurie?"

She stiffened, readying herself for a new battle. She turned her head, determined to stand firm against the triumphant arrogance she expected to see in his face. Instead, she found herself facing a man who watched her intently, his dark eyes full of concern, not triumph. Lowering her gaze, she saw that he'd wrapped a towel around his midsection. The unexpected concession to her modesty brought ridiculously inappropriate tears to her eyes.

He leaned closer, but didn't touch her. "Dry your tears, *cara*. This is a beginning for us, not an ending. I want you to sing and laugh and make love to me until you can't remember what sorrow is. I want you to be with me. Always."

She shook her head. "You'd be giving up too much. I can't let you ruin your life for me."

"Ruin my life?" He straightened and stared down at her like she was out of her mind. "Is that what you think?"

"Well, yes," she said, surprised by his reaction.

"*¡Dios!*" he cried, glancing skyward. "You send me a crazy woman to love." Shaking his head, he fixed his gaze once more on Laurie. "My life was nothing before you and Adam. Oh, I had friends and family and . . . well, I had that, too, but nothing mattered." He raised his hand and touched the center of his chest. "Here, where it counts, there was nothing."

Laurie tried to speak, but she couldn't get out the words. She seemed frozen, struck dumb by the magnitude of what he was telling her. Emotions she couldn't even begin to describe surged through her like water down an ever-narrowing river. The force of the deluge washed away her old life, cutting a new path through her soul—a new future.

He continued, his words thickening with honeyed desire. "You said you loved me, and gave me one of the most precious gifts a woman can give a man—her first passion. But I want more than one night. I want tonight, and tomorrow, and all the rest of your tomorrows. I want your promise that you'll stay with me, *cara*. Always."

At that moment the fickle *Dulcinea* performed her own kind of matchmaking. Another swell rolled past the boat, tilting the deck slightly, making Laurie lose her balance. She fell forward, tumbling directly against Gabe's chest. He smelled like the sea, and where she touched him, she burned.

"Honestly," she said shakily, "even your 'bloody boat' seems to think we should be together."

"It's what you think that matters," he said softly. He stood still, making no move to hold her, or embrace her. "Will you promise to stay with me, *cara*?"

She lifted her chin and saw shadows in his face that had nothing to do with the setting sun. There were depths to him she didn't know, depths she perhaps would never know. It didn't matter. She knew he needed her love as desperately as she needed his. Right or wrong they were part of each other, each a half of a whole. She was light to his shadow, softness to his strength. She reached up and twined her fingers through his damp hair, bringing his lips to hers. "Till death us do part, my dear pirate."

His kiss demolished what was left of her senses. Hot and urgent, it fed off the frustrated passion that had been building in both of them for over a week. Small sounds escaped her throat, encouraging him, igniting him. He tugged down her dress, covering her exposed breasts with his practiced hands, and later with his plundering mouth. Frantic with need she tried to shove the dress past her waist, but she couldn't get it past her hips. "Oh hell, I can't—"

She got no further. Gabe took control, easing her to the deck in a single fluid motion. Breathing raggedly, he pushed the full skirt up around her waist and slid his hand beneath her panties, stroking her intimate folds. Every inch of her blossomed into exquisite fire. She moved against his hand, seducing him with her own desire. She heard his sharp gasp of surprise, and knew she'd pleased him. In a smooth move of her own she reached up and stripped away his towel.

He was magnificent. Fully aroused, clothed only in shadows, he seemed more animal than man, driven by primal needs, savage appetites. Ancient hungers rose in her as well. She tried to speak, to tell him that she loved and wanted him as much as he clearly wanted her, but she couldn't manage anything more than his name. "Gabe," she cried softly. "Oh Gabe."

"My love," he breathed, making the words a prayer. Pushed past the edge, he ripped away the last barrier between them, and parted her legs. He entered her completely, filling her with the pulsing evidence of his love. She arched to welcome his intimate invasion, knowing their bodies were only confirming what their hearts had already discovered—that they were one spirit, one soul. And as the stars began to wink into existence above them, they wordlessly pledged each other eternity.

"Las Vegas?" Laurie stopped securing the mainsail to the boom and stared at Gabe in disbelief. "You want us to go to Las Vegas?"

"Sure," Gabe replied. He tied off the final knot, then looked out over the quiet marina, all but deserted in this early-morning hour. "Vegas is a great town. I'll miss the water, of course, but we've got to be practical—"

"Practical? Gabe, moving to a spotlight city like Las Vegas is about as impractical as it gets." She shook her head, smiling indulgently at her well-meaning fiancé. "We've got to move to a small town. An inconspicuous town."

"A boring town," Gabe added. "*Cara*, we can get just as lost in an exciting city as a dull one. And there's a great school system for Adam."

"Right. Blackjack Elementary," she said, laughing. "I'm not going to have my son—"

"Our son," he corrected, covering her hand with his.

Our son. Joy lit her from within, brighter by far

than the sun dappling the marina waters. She curled
her fingers around his, feeling his energy flowing into
her, gaining strength from his strength. She glanced
up into his handsome, dear face, remembering how
she'd woken in his arms and how they'd made love in
the light of the rising sun. Only yesterday her future
had seemed like an empty road, leading nowhere.
Gabe's love had given her life purpose and direction,
paved that road with gold.

"Laurie."

The unexpected sound of her name in the dead
quiet marina startled Laurie. She turned, and saw Uncle Carlos standing on the dock near *Dulcinea*'s bow.
He was dressed in his characteristically sophisticated
style, in a double-breasted dove-gray suit that perfectly complemented his silver mane. But despite his
coolly elegant appearance, his eyes were clouded with
worry and his jaw was drawn tight with strain. For the
first time since she'd known him, Carlos looked his
age.

Gabe leaned forward, clearly surprised to see his
uncle appear in an all-but-deserted marina. "*Tío?*"

He shook his head, looking miserable. "My dear
children, you must understand that I had no choice."

"No choice? *Tío*, what are you talking about?"

But Carlos didn't need to answer. Laurie was already staring past him, her gaze captured by another
man who walked toward them along the deserted
dock, his heavy steps clattering harshly on the
wooden boards. It had been years, but she still re-

membered his hard, uncompromising features, and the military cadence of his stride. She'd seen his face in her nightmares too often to forget.

Maddox, the head of TechniKon's security division.

FOURTEEN

". . . no choice," she heard Carlos saying. "He saw you on the TV footage and followed you here. If I hadn't intercepted him, he would have gone to the police."

Laurie barely listened. Instead she watched Maddox, her hope growing weaker as he got closer. Though he was still yards away, she could see he hadn't changed much with the passing years. He'd lost some of his hair, and gained some bulk around his middle, but neither had diminished his merciless superiority, or the cruel slant of his oh-so-pleasant smile. Maddox didn't just enjoy his job—he relished it. Just the thought of him getting his cruel, ruthless hands on her innocent son . . .

"Adam," she said weakly. "Carlos, is Adam—?"

"Safe," the old man assured her. "Yoli's taken him to a friend's house. TechniKon would have to tear apart the whole barrio to find him. But if you are to

206

save yourself, you must follow my lead, and trust me to—"

"Trust you?" Laurie cried, almost choking on the word. "You lead Maddox straight to me, and you expect me to trust you?"

Gabe's strong arm circled her shoulders. "*Cara*, listen to him. *Tío* knows how to play the game of deception."

"Is he the only one?" Frightened and confused, she turned to Gabe, and stared at him as if she were seeing him for the first time. "Last night I should have been with Adam, protecting him. But instead I let you kidnap me and . . ." She shook her head, consumed by guilt and tortured fury. "Was it just a coincidence, Gabe? Was it?"

He winced as if she'd struck him. "You can't believe that. Not after everything we said to each other, everything we did and felt." He grasped her shoulders, forcing her to face him. "Laurie, you can't believe that I'd betray—"

"Long time no see, Dr. Lawrence."

She stiffened, remembering the harsh voice from her past, and her nightmares. Memories came rushing back—the claustrophobic basement room, the ticking wall clock, the throat-scarring smell of stale cigarette smoke, and the waiting, the endless waiting. It was hard not to listen for the sound of wings. She closed her eyes, overwhelmed by the memories of terror and despair.

"Courage, *cara*," Gabe whispered, his warm breath brushing her ear. "I promised I'd never let anyone hurt you or Adam, and I mean to keep that promise."

Laurie's eyes flew open. She met Gabe's dark glance and saw the stark reality of his love for her burning in their depths. It was an intrinsic part of him, just as loving him was a part of her. Mountains might crumble, the sun might cease to shine, but she'd never again doubt the truth of his love. She raised her hand to his cheek. "Gabe, I'm sorry. I should never have doubted—"

"Dr. Lawrence!" Maddox yelled, "if you're not off that boat in one minute, I'm coming up to get you."

Gabe lifted his head and yelled over Laurie's shoulder. "Set one foot on this boat, amigo, and you'll lose it!"

"Gentlemen!" Carlos intervened. "This isn't getting us anywhere. Now, I'm sure if we all sit down and discuss this sensibly, we can come to a solution."

"The only solution," Maddox stated, "is for Dr. Lawrence to give back the property she stole. If she does, we might consider dropping the charges against her. *Might*," he emphasized with a singularly unpleasant smile.

Prison, Laurie thought. That's where Maddox would send her if she didn't hand Adam over to him. Correction—that's where he was *going* to have to send her, because she had no intention of handing over her son. Six years ago she'd brained Maddox with a folding chair rather than give up her son. She hadn't been the docile little scientist he'd expected her to be then, and she certainly wasn't now. "You can take your *solution*, Maddox, and go straight to—"

"Gabe's office," Carlos interrupted. "My nephew's office is nearby. I'll take you there. We can discuss the matter in private there—unless all of you would like to continue yelling our personal business in an open marina."

Maddox grumbled, but he clearly didn't want the particulars about Adam voiced in public. "All right, Ramirez, I'll meet you there. But don't get any ideas about leaving, Dr. Lawrence. One word from me and the police will be covering every bus depot and airport in this city. And your friends," he added, looking pointedly at Gabe and Carlos, "will end up working on a fishing boat back in Cuba."

Maddox stalked away with Carlos following. Gabe's uncle looked just as distressed and harried as ever, but at the last moment he glanced back, and gave the two of them a decidedly mischievous wink.

"I knew it," Gabe cried, wrapping Laurie in a fierce hug. "That wily old man is up to something. Everything's going to be fine."

"Not this time," Laurie said quietly. Enveloped in the safety of his arms, she could almost believe that this horrible nightmare she'd been living would have a fairy-tale ending. But she knew it was a hopeless wish, as splendid and as impossible as the wonderful future they'd planned together on this boat last night. "Gabe, TechniKon has me dead to rights. When I don't give them Adam, they're going to send me to prison, and no scheme of *Tío*'s is going to stop them."

She swallowed, tried to hold back the tears of frustration that pricked her eyes. "TechniKon will win in the end. They always do."

For several minutes Gabe said nothing. He just held her, stroking her bright hair, and listening to the cry of the sea gulls as they dipped and rose over the sun-dappled waves. Everything about the morning spoke of newness and life, as if God had cut this moment from the fabric of time just for them. Laurie laid her cheek against the hollow of his shoulder, surrendering to his strength, his courage, and his love. TechniKon might take away her freedom, but they could never rob her of her real treasure—the love she felt for this special, caring man.

"*Cara*," he said at last, "I asked you once if you trusted me. You said it wasn't a matter of trust, but of reality. Well, this is our reality." He took her hand and laced his strong, blunt fingers through her delicate ones. "We are bound together, you and I. And nothing in our pasts, or our futures, will ever change that."

"But I'm afraid for you," she confessed. "Maddox wasn't kidding about that Cuban fishing boat. He has powerful contacts in the government—powerful enough to get both you and your uncle deported. TechniKon is no one to mess with."

She expected him to agree with her, or at least to promise to be cautious. Instead, he threw back his head and gave a lusty laugh that rang through the morning air. "That may be so," he said, flashing her his buccaneer grin, "but neither are the Ramirezes."

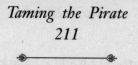

Laurie reread the paper Carlos had just handed her, hoping that she was mistaken. But the ponderously legal wording remained the same. *The party of the first part will return all existing procured property to the party of the second part, in exchange for the cessation of criminal prosecution. . . .*

She glanced across Gabe's desk, to the office chairs where jowl-jawed Maddox and elegant Carlos sat side by side, looking like the most mismatched pair in the world. But perhaps they had more in common than she realized. *Like the devil and the deep blue sea.* "*Tío*, I can't sign this agreement. You know I can't."

"But you must, my dear," Carlos said, appearing genuinely concerned. "If you do not, Mr. Maddox has assured me that TechniKon will press charges, and you could end up going to prison."

"There's no *could* about it," Maddox sneered.

Laurie flinched at the undisguised threat. She remembered that sneer so well from her days at TechniKon. Maddox had always been a bully, taking great pleasure in intimidating those weaker than himself. She hated the fact that he thought he had the power to intimidate her. She hated it more that he was right. She swallowed, feeling her courage flagging. "I can't sign," she said weakly.

"Fine," Maddox replied. He reached down and picked up his briefcase, and pulled out a cellular phone. "I assume 911 works even in this godforsaken neighborhood—hey!"

Gabe, who'd been sitting on the windowsill, reached out and plucked the phone from the security chief's hand. With quiet menace he stated, "I do not believe the lady has made up her mind yet. A gentleman would wait until she has done so."

"A gentleman might," Maddox agreed, "*if* she were a lady."

Laurie never even saw Gabe move. The next thing she knew he'd pulled Maddox out of his seat by his collar, easily overpowering the man despite his superior bulk. "You will apologize to Dr. Lawrence."

"Like hell. I'll see you get adjoining cells."

"Gabriel, release him at once," cried Carlos, leaping to his feet. He pulled apart the battling men, and managed, with little effort, to place himself physically between Maddox and Laurie. "Do you see what will happen, my dear?" he said, his voice uncharacteristically uncertain. "You must sign, for the good of us all. You must trust me when I say you will not regret it."

Trust me. Ultimately that's what it came down to, whether she trusted Gabe and Carlos with her safety. And, more importantly, with the safety of her son. Trust had never come easily to her, even at the best of times. And in the face of Maddox's threats, it was harder for her to trust than ever.

She looked up, and caught Gabe's hooded glance. Their eyes met only for an instant, yet it was enough for Laurie to see the bright snap of hope burning in their sable depths. Courage, they told her. *I will never let anyone harm you.*

The cold uncertainty of the past melted like ice in the Miami sun. *It's not just me you're up against this time, Maddox. It's Gabe, and Carlos, and every Ramirez who ever sailed the high seas.* She took the paper and signed it without hesitation, then handed it to Carlos.

"That's fine, my dear. Now, just hand over that research of yours to Mr. Maddox."

Laurie glanced between Gabe and his uncle in alarm. "But . . . I burned the research."

"You did?" Carlos said, looking genuinely surprised. "Well, that certainly makes things difficult. This contract clearly states that *existing* property will be returned. But if the property no longer exists—"

"Hold it," Maddox said, grabbing the paper from Carlos's grasp. "You may have burned the research, but you've still got the boy." He leaned on the desk, and looked at Laurie with a steel-cold stare. "I don't know what you think you're up to, but it will take more than a piece of paper to keep you out of prison. We want the boy, Dr. Lawrence. And if you don't give him to us, we'll—"

"Excuse me," Carlos interrupted, "what boy are you referring to?"

"Her boy," Maddox snapped. "The one she passes off as her son."

Carlos's eyes narrowed like a wolf going in for the kill. "But Mr. Maddox, my nephew and I have known Dr. Lawrence since she arrived in Little Havana, and I can assure you she has no son."

❖————————————————❖

For several seconds Laurie forgot how to breathe. She gaped at Carlos, amazed that he could even contemplate telling such an outrageous lie, much less expect to get away with it. She knew the cunning trial lawyer had pulled off some pretty amazing cons in the past, but this one could send him straight to prison as a criminal accomplice. Her eyes traveled to Gabe, expecting to see her own sentiments mirrored in his expression.

Instead, she saw him grinning at Carlos with unabashed admiration and pleasure. He and his uncle were cut from the same bolt of cloth—the Ramirez bolt. Dammit, those two were going to swashbuckle their way straight to the penitentiary if she didn't do something. She turned to Maddox, determined to put an end to Carlos's and Gabe's involvement, for their own good. "Maddox, this is between you and me. I don't want anyone invol—"

She stopped as Gabe came to her side and gave her what appeared to be a supportive pat on the back. In actuality, he expertly pressed his fingers against a certain spot at the base of her neck, a spot he'd made considerable use of the night before. As a result, the rest of Laurie's sentence died in a strangled gasp.

"You're harassing my client," Carlos stated, effectively drawing Maddox's attention away from Laurie. "See what you're doing to the poor woman. *¡Concho!* She can barely breathe."

"She'll lose more than her breath when I'm

through with her," Maddox promised. "Nice try, Dr. Lawrence, but it won't work. I've had my men checking the neighborhood. All I have to do is find someone who will testify that you have a son, and—"

He was interrupted by the ring of his cellular phone. "That's probably my men reporting now," he said smugly as he snapped the phone open and lifted it to his ear. "Maddox."

Laurie glanced down at her tightly clenched hands, her heart sinking. Gabe and Carlos might lie for her, but there was no way she could expect the whole neighborhood to perjure themselves on her behalf. They had families to think about, lives and reputations. She and Adam were virtually strangers. She wouldn't blame any of them for telling Maddox's men whatever they wanted to know.

"What? But that's impossible!"

Laurie's chin shot up, her gaze riveting on the sputtering Maddox. For the first time since she'd known him, the security chief looked totally bewildered.

"But someone must have seen him," Maddox barked into the receiver. "What about the apartment manager? . . . Okay, then try the woman who runs the grocery store Lawrence worked at, or the other kids on the block . . . You have?"

Maddox's face grew beet-red. He grunted a curt order to his unseen subordinate to keep trying, then snapped the receiver shut. "I don't know how you managed it," he stated, glancing between Laurie and her defenders, "but my men can't find anyone who'll testify that the doctor has a son. It appears we've reached a Mexican—no, make that a *Cuban* standoff." He rubbed his jowled cheek, and studied Gabe and Carlos with something that looked unpleasantly like admiration. "All right, tell me how much. How much for the boy? People always talk if the price is right. And TechniKon can make it very right."

Gabe's oath scorched Laurie's ears. He and Carlos moved as one, facing down Maddox with undisguised loathing.

"This isn't about money," Gabe stated. "I don't think it ever was. Laurie's experiment, no matter how lucrative, could hardly make up for the time and money you've spent hunting her down over the years. It's not so much the boy you want, as the fact that you want to take him from Laurie. You want revenge for her getting the better of you. That's it, isn't it?"

Maddox looked as if he'd been punched in the gut. Stuttering, he raised the paper Laurie'd just signed in front of Gabe's face. "This contract entitles me to—"

With a swipe of his hand Gabe pushed the paper away. "You are entitled to nothing! You persecute a defenseless woman, and call it your right. Well, I have news for you. Laurie is no longer defenseless. She has friends now—people who love her."

Laurie trembled, consumed by the depth of his belief in her. The light of his love blinded her, shining into the dark places of her life, replacing fear and despair with truth and hope. He was right about Maddox—the man's obsession with her and Adam spoke of revenge more than justice. But until he'd said it aloud, she'd never understood, never realized that it was Maddox, not her, who was the true criminal. "Gabe," she said, putting all the love and trust she felt for him in his name.

The intense moment was shattered by the gunshot sound of a briefcase being slammed shut. Latching shut the locks, Maddox picked up the case, and started from the room. "This isn't over—not by a long shot. I know damn well that kid's here somewhere. My men will keep looking for him, and when they find him, I'll—"

"And what," Carlos interrupted, "will your stockholders think of that, I wonder?"

Maddox stopped walking. "The stockholders?"

"Yes, the people whose money supports TechniKon—the people whose money you're spending while you continue this hunt for the boy." Carlos paused, taking a moment to brush a spot from his spotless sleeve. "Dr. Lawrence believes that they would not be too happy to learn of TechniKon's, uhm, dabbling in genetic cloning. Isn't that right, Laurie?"

"Well, yes," Laurie agreed. What was *Tío* up to now?

Maddox apparently wondered the same thing. "The only thing the stockholders care about is the fact that the doctor stole TechniKon property."

"I think you are mistaken," Carlos said, his voice as smooth as polished glass. "They are people with hearts and minds, and when they learn what you have done to this woman—how you hounded her for years for the 'crime' of loving a child—I fear it will not sit well with them." He glanced at the security chief, his lips curving up in a scoundrel's smile. "And they will find out, Mr. Maddox. My *friends* may not be so highly placed as TechniKon's associates, but they know how to whisper secrets into the right ears. If you continue this 'hunt,' I promise you that the stockholders will learn the truth about your *property*. Heads will roll, Maddox. Yours included."

Laurie held her breath, and knew by the tautness in Gabe's muscles that he was doing the same. She saw *Tío*'s plan clearly now—a trade-off between Maddox's job and the safety of herself and her son. There was a chance it might work, if Maddox backed down. But, as far as Laurie knew, TechniKon's head angel had never backed down from anything.

"She stole TechniKon's property," Maddox growled.

Carlos fired back. "And you stole God's when you sought to make life where there was none. Tell me which, my friend, is the greater crime."

Electric silence charged the air. Laurie swallowed, her heart beating so hard, she was amazed it didn't shatter her ribs. She couldn't meet Gabe's eyes, but she held on to him like a lifeline, drawing on his buried strength to keep her sane. Their future, the bright and wonderful life they'd promised each other last night, was once again within their grasp. But it could slip away so easily, so very easily. She'd be left with a broken heart and an empty future . . . a handful of dark feathers . . .

She turned her head, but not toward Gabe or Carlos. Instead, she stared straight at Maddox, facing him squarely for the first time in six years. Looking into his unforgiving eyes, she felt as if she were again back in that windowless room, with its ticking clock and cigarette stench. With its soul-killing fear.

Six years ago she'd looked away from those eyes, unable to brave their cruel superiority. But six years ago she hadn't met Gabe, and hadn't learned to rely on his love as she did now. Six years ago she'd been alone, friendless. Now, because of Carlos and the generous people of Calle Ocho, and most especially because of the strong and tender man who held her in his arms, she knew she'd never be alone again. She faced down Maddox, making him see that she was not the frightened scientist that he'd known years ago, and that she was not and never would be intimidated by his bullying. *You've lost, Maddox,* her mind whispered. *Even if you send me to prison, you've lost.*

And, on some level, Maddox must have understood, because without a word he opened his briefcase and pulled out the contract, and tore it in half.

EPILOGUE

The engagement party was over. Berta's comfortable, rambling house, which had been packed to the rafters with relatives and well-wishers throughout the long afternoon and evening, now lay still and silent in the summer moonlight. Minutes before the last of the guests had been ushered out the front door, leaving behind a volley of good wishes, and a Mount Everest pile of dirty dishes. And in the back of the house a couple slipped secretly into the deserted den, cherishing a stolen moment of togetherness at the end of a hectic day.

"I should be helping Berta and Yoli with the dishes," Laurie confessed.

"The dishes can wait. I can't," Gabe growled as he wrapped her in his arms. "*Dios*, it's been a lifetime since I've held you."

"It's been ten minutes," Laurie said as she snuggled against his chest. "You hugged me during your third cousin Eduardo's last toast to our health and happiness."

"I'd be healthier and happier if Eduardo had stopped toasting us and left with the others." He smoothed her hair, letting the soft strands drift between his fingers. "I know our future, *cara*. I've known it since the first moment I saw you."

"I think I did too," she confessed, raising her eyes to meet his loving gaze. "Adam thought you were an avenging angel. He wasn't far wrong."

She lifted her hand to trace the strong line of his jaw and caught the glint of her new engagement ring, gleaming like a star in the darkness. A peace she'd never known filled her heart. During the past weeks Maddox and TechniKon had faded from her memory like a bad dream. Even her nightmares about the angels had disappeared, and she doubted they'd ever return. "It's really over this time, isn't it?"

"Yes," he promised, pressing a quick kiss against her hair. "My sources tell me that TechniKon hasn't made one move toward you or your son since our talk with Maddox. But even if they do, they'll have a hell of a time disproving the new identity Carlos established for Adam as a distant Ramirez cousin. And they'll have an even tougher time once we've legally adopted him. Besides, TechniKon's going to be dealing with other worries for a while."

"What other worries?"

"Carlos isn't the only one with connections. I told certain—uhm—associates I knew from my days on the force that TechniKon's directors were 'dipping into the till.' Since these people are heavily invested in TechniKon's subsidiaries, they'll be urging the directors to clean up their act. *Strongly* urging," he added with a devilish smile.

"You're a dangerous man, Gabe Ramirez," Laurie commented without a trace of fear. "I can see I'm going to have my hands full for the next sixty or seventy years."

He pulled her into the crook of his arm. She went willingly, knowing there was nowhere else on earth she'd rather be. Looking up, she saw that his smile had turned suddenly sober.

"It won't be a grand life," he warned her. "My business might never make a lot of money. You'll probably spend the rest of your life in Little Havana."

"I was planning to anyway," she said as she wrapped her arms around his waist. "I'm going to open a clinic here—a real clinic. How do you feel about having an impoverished, overworked doctor for a wife?"

"As long as it doesn't interfere with us making babies." He caught her chin in his hand, giving her a loving shake. "And I mean the *old-fashioned* way, *puchunguita*."

She laughed and started to answer him, but found her mouth commandeered for other purposes. She melted into his embrace, returning his kiss with equal passion, equal joy. A lifetime of loving stretched before them like a shining road, free of the fears and shadows of the past, leading only to bright tomorrows.

The shining road was momentarily interrupted as the door opened, admitting Adam. "Geez, I've been looking everywhere for you guys," he said as his blinking eyes adjusted to the den's darkness. "What are you doing?"

"I'm kissing your mother," Gabe answered. "Is that all right with you?"

"I suppose I'll have to get used to it," Adam sighed with a six-year-old's long-suffering tolerance for the baffling behavior of adults. "Anyway, I've got a question. Yoli showed me this," he explained, handing Gabe an oversize Tarot card. "She said it was you."

Reluctantly releasing his fiancée, Gabe stepped over to the wall switch and turned on the light. Settling his hip on the edge of the desk, he studied the card, noting that it pictured a man on a throne, surrounded by an abundance of treasures. Across the top was written the word "Emperor." Gabe smiled slightly, recalling the day Yoli had come rushing into his office, crying that she'd found the "Empress."

He heard a rustle near his elbow. Laurie sat down on the desk beside him, leaning against his shoulder as she, too, examined the card. The next thing he knew Adam hopped up onto the desk on his other side, and also fixed his gaze on the card. Gabe glanced from one bent head to the other, thinking that no man on earth had ever been surrounded by such richness. The treasures of his ancestors couldn't begin to compare to the love he felt for these two people, or the love they felt for him. "Yoli is right," he told Adam truthfully. "This lucky man is me."

Laurie raised her head, meeting his eyes with an indigo gaze so full of love, it nearly burst his heart. But Adam was far less sure. He took the card, scratching his head in puzzlement. "I don't get it. This guy doesn't look anything like a pirate."

THE EDITOR'S CORNER

The end of summer means back to school and cooler weather, but here at LOVESWEPT temperatures are rising with four sensational romances to celebrate the beginning of autumn. You'll thrill to the sexiest heroes and cheer for the most spirited heroines as they discover the power of passion. They're sure to heat up your reading hours with their wonderful, sensuous tales.

Leading our lineup is the marvelously talented Debra Dixon with **MOUNTAIN MYSTIC**, LOVESWEPT # 706. Joshua Logan has always been able to read anyone's emotions, but he can't figure Victoria Bennett out—maybe because his longing for the beautiful midwife is so unexpected! He'd come home to the mountains seeking refuge from a world that demanded more than he could give; why now did he have to meet a woman who awakened his need to touch and be touched? Debra weaves a moving story of trust and healing that you won't forget.

Donna Kauffman invites you to meet a **BOUNTY HUNTER**, LOVESWEPT # 707. Kane Hawthorne was hired to locate a runaway wife, but when he finds Elizabeth Lawson, he knows he has to claim her as his own! A desperate woman who dares trust no one, she tries to keep him from making her enemies his, but Kane insists on fighting her demons. And she has no choice but to cherish her savage hero until his own ghosts are silenced. With this electrifying romance Donna proves that nobody does it better when it comes to writing about a dangerous and sexy man.

Cindy Gerard's newest book will keep you awake long **INTO THE NIGHT**, LOVESWEPT # 708. It began as a clever gimmick to promote a radio show for lovers, but the spirited sparring between Jessie Fox and Tony Falcone is so believable, listeners demand to know more of their steamy romance! Jessie vows it is impossible for this gorgeous younger man to want her with the fire she sees burning in his eyes —until the brash Falcon sets a seductive trap his Fox can't escape. Cindy's irresistible blend of humor and playful passion creates a memorable couple you will cherish.

The ever popular Peggy Webb has written her most sensual and heartbreaking novel yet with **ONLY HIS TOUCH**, LOVESWEPT # 709. For years Kathleen Shaw's body had danced to the music of Hunter La Farge's mouth and hands, but when the beautiful ballerina loses everything she'd lived for in a shocking accident, the untamed adventurer is the last man she wants to face. Twice before he'd lost the woman who shared his soul, but now the fierce panther who had claimed her for all time must set her free to recapture her dream. This is Peggy at her best —keep a box of tissues handy!

I'd like to take this opportunity to share with you some exciting news. I have been promoted to Deputy Publisher here at Bantam and will consequently be managing all aspects of the Bantam adult hardcover, trade, and mass-market paperback publishing program. I will continue to oversee women's fiction, but most of the hands-on work will be handled by Senior Editor Beth de Guzman, Assistant Editor Shauna Summers, and Administrative Editor Gina Iemolo. Of course, none of this changes our team's continuing goal to bring you the best in contemporary romantic fiction written by the most talented and loved authors in the genre.

Happy reading!

With warmest wishes,

Nita Taublib

Nita Taublib

Deputy Publisher

P.S. Don't miss the exciting women's novels from Bantam that are coming your way in September— **ADAM'S FALL** is the paperback reprint of the classic romantic novel from *New York Times* bestselling author Sandra Brown; **THE LAST BACHELOR**, from nationally bestselling author Betina Krahn, is a spectacularly entertaining battle of the sexes set in Victorian England; **PRINCE OF WOLVES**, by Susan Krinard, is a spellbinding new romance of mystery, magic, and forbidden passion in the tradition of Linda Lael Miller; and **WHISPERED LIES** is the latest novel from Christy Cohen, about two intimate strangers divided by dangerous secrets, broken vows, and misplaced passions. We'll be giving you a sneak peek at these terrific books in next month's LOVE-SWEPTs. And immediately following this page look for a preview of the exciting romances from Bantam that are *available now!*

Don't miss these electrifying books by
your favorite Bantam authors

On sale in July:
MIDNIGHT WARRIOR
by Iris Johansen

BLUE MOON
by Luanne Rice

VELVET
by Jane Feather

WITCH DANCE
by Peggy Webb

Winner of *Romantic Times's*
Career Achievement Award

Iris Johansen

THE *NEW YORK TIMES* BESTSELLING
AUTHOR OF
THE BELOVED SCOUNDREL

MIDNIGHT WARRIOR

*From the author who has been lauded as "the Mistress of
Romantic Fantasy" comes a passionate new tale of danger,
adventure, and romance that sweeps from a Saxon strong-
hold to a lovers' bower in the cool, jade-green forests of
Wales. . . .*

Brynn hesitated for a moment and then said reluctantly, "This is a bad place. Can't you feel it?"

"Feel what?"

"If you cannot feel it, I can't explain. I just want to
be gone from here." She paused and then whispered,
"Please."

He looked at her in surprise. "This must mean a
good deal to you. You're more given to commands
than pleas."

She didn't answer.

"What if I give you what you wish?" He lowered his voice to silky softness. "Will you give me a gift in turn?"

"I've given you a gift. Your friend Malik is alive. Isn't that enough for you?"

"It should be."

"But it isn't?"

"Malik will tell you I don't know the meaning of enough. The prize just over the horizon is always the sweetest."

"So you reach out and take it," she said flatly.

"Or barter for it. I prefer the latter. It suits my merchant's soul. I suppose Malik has told you that I'm more trader than knight?"

"No, he said you were the son of a king and capable of being anything you wanted to be."

"Which obviously did not impress you."

"Why should it? It does not matter their station, men are all the same."

He smiled. "Certainly in some aspects. You didn't answer. Will you barter with me?"

"I have nothing with which to barter."

"You're a woman. A woman always has great bartering power."

She straightened her shoulders and turned to look directly at him. "You mean you wish me to be your whore."

His lips tightened. "Your words lack a certain delicacy."

"They do not lack truth." She looked down into the pot. "You wish me to part my limbs and let you rut like a beast of the forest. I wonder you even seek to bargain. You think me your slave. Isn't a slave to be used?"

"Yes," he said curtly. "A slave is to work and give

pleasure. And you're right, I don't have to bargain with you. I can do what I wish."

"I'm glad that is clear." She stirred faster, harder. "Shall we go into the tent now? Or perhaps you wish to take me in front of all your soldiers? I'd be grateful if you'd have the kindness to let me finish preparing this salve that is making your friend well and healthy. But if I seem unreasonable, you must only tell me and I will—"

"Be silent!" His teeth clenched, he added, "I've never met a woman with such a—"

"I'm only being humble and obliging. Isn't that what you want of me?"

"I want—" He stopped and then said thickly, "I'm not certain what I want . . . yet. When I do, I'll be sure you're made fully aware of it."

"Rice has an elegant style, a sharp eye and a real warmth. In her hands families—and their values—seem worth cherishing."
—*San Francisco Chronicle*

BLUE MOON

BY

Luanne Rice

BLUE MOON is a moving novel of a family that discovers the everyday magic of life and the extraordinary power of love. The New York Times *has already praised it as "a rare combination of realism and romance."* Entertainment Weekly *has simply called it "brilliant," and* People *has raved that it is "eloquent . . . a moving and complete tale of the complicated phenomenon we call family."*

Here is a look at this powerful novel. . . .

After two weeks at sea, Billy Medieros was heading home. He usually loved this part of the trip, when the hold was full of fish and his crew was happy because they knew their share of the catch would be high, and they'd all sleep in their own beds that night. He drove the *Norboca*—the best boat in his father-in-law's fleet —around Minturn Ledge, and Mount Hope came into view.

Billy stood at the wheel. The tide had been against

him, and he knew he had missed Cass. She would have left work by now, was probably already home cooking supper. He could picture her at the stove, stirring something steamy, her summer dress sticking damply to her breasts and hips. His wife had the body of a young sexpot. Other guys at sea would pray to Miss July, but Billy would look at pictures of Cass, her coppery curls falling across her face, her blue eyes sexy and mysterious, delicate fingers cupping her full breasts, offering them to the camera. She had given him a Minolta for his last birthday, but for his real present she had posed nude.

Lately, to Billy, Cass had seemed more real in his bunk at sea than she was at home. In person, Cass looked the same, she smelled the same, but she seemed absent, somehow. Raising Josie changed her every day, and Billy resisted the transformation. He missed his wife.

He was nearly home. His eyes roved the church spires, the wooden piers clawing the harbor, American flags flapping from the yacht club and every hotel roof, white yachts rocking on the waves, two trawlers heading out. He waved to the skippers, both of whom he had fished with before. Manuel Vega waved back, a beer in his hand.

Billy couldn't stand skippers who drank onboard. It set a bad example for the crew. You had to stay keen every second. Billy had seen terrible things happen to fishermen who weren't paying attention—fingers lost to a winch handle, a skull split open by a boom. On Billy's first trip out with his father-in-law, Jimmy Keating, a crewmate with both hands busy setting nets had bitten down on a skinny line to hold it in place, and a gust of wind had yanked out six of his top teeth.

Stupid. Billy had no patience for stupid crew

members, and dulling your senses with alcohol, at sea on a fifty-foot boat, was stupid.

"Docking!" Billy yelled, and four guys ran up from below. John Barnard, Billy's first mate for this trip, stood with Billy at the bridge. They had gone to high school together; they'd fished as a team hundreds of times. They never confided in each other, but they had an easygoing way of passing time for long stretches.

Strange, maybe, considering that John Barnard was the only man Billy had ever felt jealous of. Cass liked him too much.

Not that anything had ever happened. But Billy knew she'd get that look in her eyes whenever she was going to see John. Before Christmas parties, Holy Ghost Society Dances, even goddamn PTA meetings. Cass was a flirt, for sure; it only made Billy that much prouder she belonged to him.

Cass and John had dated a couple of times after high school, when Cass had wanted to marry Billy and Billy had been too dumb to ask. Billy, delivering scallops to Lobsterville one night, had met Cass's mother in the kitchen.

"I want to show you something," Mary Keating said. She began leading Billy into the dining room.

"I can't go in there," Billy said, sniffing his sleeve. His rubber boots tracked fragments of scallop shells.

"You'd better, if you don't want to lose her," Mary said. Five-two in her red high heels, Mary Keating had a husky smoker's voice and the drive of a Detroit diesel. Standing in the kitchen doorway, blocking waiters, she pointed across the dining room. There, at a table for two, framed by a picture window overlooking a red sun setting over Mount Hope harbor, were Cass and John having dinner together.

Bonnie and Nora, in their waitress uniforms, hovered nearby.

John was tall, with sandy-brown hair and a movie-hero profile, and the way he and Cass were leaning across the table, smiling into each other's eyes, made Billy want to vault across the bar and smash John's face into his plate. He left without a word, but the incident brought Billy to his senses; two months later, he and Cass were married.

Billy pulled back on the throttle as they passed the No Wake buoy.

"Almost there," John said.

"Can I grab a ride with you?" Billy asked. The Barnards, like most fishing families, lived in Alewives Park.

"Sure," John said. "No problem."

The deck hands checked the dock lines, then stood along the port rail, waiting to jump ashore. Billy threw the engine into reverse, then eased the boat ahead. She bumped hard once, hard again, and then settled into a gentle sway.

In the bestselling tradition of
Amanda Quick, a spectacular new
historical romance from the nationally
bestselling

Jane Feather

"An author to treasure."
—*Romantic Times*

VELVET

Clad in black velvet and posing as a widowed French com-
tesse, Gabrielle de Beaucaire had returned to England for
one purpose only—to ruin the man responsible for her
young lover's death. But convincing the forbidding Na-
thaniel Praed, England's greatest spymaster, that she
would make the perfect agent for his secret service would
not be easy. And even after Gabrielle had lured the devas-
tatingly attractive lord to her bed, she would have to con-
tend with his distrust—and with the unexpected hunger
that his merest touch aroused. . . .

It was a bright clear night, the air crisp, the stars
sharp in the limitless black sky. He flung open the
window, leaning his elbows on the sill, looking out
over the expanse of smooth lawn where frost glittered

under the starlight. It would be a beautiful morning for the hunt.

He climbed back into bed and blew out his candle.

He heard the rustling of the woodbine almost immediately. His hand slipped beneath his pillow to his constant companion, the small silver-mounted pistol. He lay very still, every muscle held in waiting, his ears straining into the darkness. The small scratching, rustling sounds continued, drawing closer to the open window. Someone was climbing the thick ancient creeper clinging to the mellow brick walls of the Jacobean manor house.

His hand closed more firmly over the pistol and he hitched himself up on one elbow, his eyes on the square of the window, waiting.

Hands competently gripped the edge of the windowsill, followed by a dark head. The nocturnal visitor swung a leg over the sill and hitched himself upright, straddling the sill.

"Since you've only just snuffed your candle, I'm sure you're still awake," Gabrielle de Beaucaire said into the dark, still room. "And I'm sure you have a pistol, so please don't shoot, it's only me."

Nathaniel was rarely taken by surprise and was a master at concealing it on those rare occasions. On this occasion, however, his training deserted him.

"*Only!*" he exclaimed. "What the hell are you doing?"

"Guess," his visitor challenged cheerfully from her perch.

"You'll have to forgive me, but I don't find guessing games amusing," he declared in clipped accents. He sat up, his pistol still in his hand, and stared at the dark shape outlined against the moonlight. That aura of trouble surrounding Gabrielle de Beaucaire had not been a figment of his imagination.

"Perhaps I should be flattered," he said icily. "Am I to assume unbridled lust lies behind the honor of this visit, madam?" His eyes narrowed.

Disconcertingly, the woman appeared to be impervious to irony. She laughed. A warm, merry sound that Nathaniel found as incongruous in the circumstances as it was disturbingly attractive.

"Not at his point, Lord Praed; but there's no saying what the future might hold." It was a mischievous and outrageous statement that rendered him temporarily speechless.

She took something out of the pocket of her britches and held it on the palm of her hand. "I'm here to present my credentials."

She swung off the windowsill and approached the bed, a sinuous figure in her black britches and glimmering white shirt.

He leaned sideways, struck flint on tinder, and re-lit the bedside candle. The dark red hair glowed in the light as she extended her hand, palm upward, toward him and he saw what she held.

It was a small scrap of black velvet cut with a ragged edge.

"Well, well." The evening's puzzles were finally solved. Lord Praed opened a drawer in the bedside table and took out a piece of tissue paper. Unfolding it, he revealed the twin of the scrap of material.

"I should have guessed," he said pensively. "Only a woman would have come up with such a fanciful idea." He took the velvet from her extended palm and fitted the ragged edge to the other piece, making a whole square. "So you're Simon's surprise. No wonder he was so secretive. But what makes you think I would ever employ a woman?"

WITCH DANCE

BY

Peggy Webb

"Ms. Webb has an inventive mind brimming with originality that makes all of her books special reading."—*Romantic Times*

An exquisite woman of ivory and jade, she'd come to Witch Dance, Oklahoma, to bring modern medicine to the native Chickasaw people. But when Dr. Kate Malone saw the magnificent Indian rising from the river, naked as sin and twice as tempting, every thought of duty was lost, drowned in a primitive wave of longing that made her tremble with desire. . . .

He was more man than she'd ever seen. And every gorgeous inch of him was within touching distance.

For all he seemed to care, he could have been bending over her in a Brooks Brothers suit.

"What impulse sent you into the river?" He squatted beside her with both hands on her shoulders, and she'd never felt skin as hot in her life.

" I thought you were drowning."

His laughter was deep and melodious, and as sensual as exotic music played in some dark corner of a dimly lit café where lovers embraced.

"I am Chickasaw," he said, as if that explained everything.

"Well, I'm human and I made a mistake." She pushed her wet hair away from her face. "Why can't you just admit you made a mistake, staying under the water so long I thought you were going to drown?"

"You were watching me?"

"No . . . yes . . ." His legs were powerful, heavily muscled, bent in such a way that the best parts of him were hidden. He leaned closer, intent on answers. How did he expect her to think straight with his leg touching hers like that? "Not deliberately," she said. "I was on a picnic. How did I know you'd be cavorting about in the river without any clothes on?"

He searched her face with eyes deep and black. Then he touched her cheeks, his strong hands exquisitely gentle.

"I'm sorry I ruined your picnic." Ever so tenderly his hands roamed over her face. Breathless, she sat beside the river, his willing captive. "You've scratched your face . . . here . . . and here."

Until that moment she hadn't known that every nerve in the body could tremble. Now she could attest to it as a medical fact.

". . . and your legs." He gave her legs the same tender attention he'd given her face. She would have sold her soul to feel his hands on her forever. "I have remedies for your injuries."

Oh, God. Would he kiss them and make them well? She almost said it.

"I can fix them . . ." How? She could barely breathe. "I'm a doctor."

"You came to Tribal Lands to practice medicine?"

"You doubt my word?"

"No. Your commitment."

"Is it because I'm white that you think I'm not committed, or because I'm female?"

"Neither, *Wictonaye.*" In one fluid movement he stood before her, smiling.

And in that moment her world changed. Colors

and light receded, faded, until there was nothing except the bold Chickasaw with his glowing, polished skin and his seductive voice that obliterated every thought, every need except the most basic . . . to die of love. Sitting on the hard ground, looking up at her nameless captor, she wanted to die in the throes of passion.

She stood on shaky, uncertain legs. Clenching her fists by her side, she faced him.

"If you're going to call me names, use English, please."

"*Wictonaye* . . . wildcat."

"I've been called worse." Would God forgive her if she left right now? Would He give her the healing touch and allow her to save lives if she forgot about her lust and focused on her mission?

She spun around, then felt his hand on her arm.

"I've been rude. It's not my way."

"Nor mine." She grinned. "Except sometimes."

"You tried to save my life, and I don't know your name."

"Kate Malone."

"Thank you for saving my life, Kate Malone." His eyes sparkled with wicked glee. She'd never known a man of such boldness . . . nor such appeal. "I'm Eagle Mingo."

"Next time you decide to play in the river, Eagle Mingo, be more careful. I might not be around to rescue you."

She marched toward the bluff, thinking it was a good exit, until he appeared beside her, still naked as sin and twice as tempting.

"You forgot your shoe." He held out one of her moccasins.

"Thanks." Lord, did he expect her to bend down

and put it on with him standing there like that? She hobbled along, half shoeless.

"And your picnic basket." He scooped it off the ground and handed it to her. Then, damned if he didn't bow like some courtly knight in shining armor.

If she ever got home, she'd have to take an aspirin and go to bed. Doctor's orders.

"Good-bye. Enjoy your"—her eyes raked him from head to toe, and she could feel her whole body getting hot—"swim."

She didn't know how she got up the bluff, but she didn't draw a good breath until she was safely at the top. He was still standing down there, looking up. She could feel his eyes on her.

Lest he think she was a total coward, she put on her other shoe, then turned and casually waved at him. At least she hoped it was casual.

Dammit all, he waved back. Facing full front. She might never recover.

And don't miss these incredible romances from Bantam Books, on sale in August:

THE LAST BACHELOR

by the nationally bestselling author

Betina Krahn

"One of the genre's most creative writers."
—*Romantic Times*

PRINCE OF WOLVES

by the sensational

Susan Krinard

A romance of mystery, magic, and forbidden passion

WHISPERED LIES

by the highly acclaimed

Christy Cohen

A novel of dangerous desires and seductive secrets

OFFICIAL RULES

To enter the sweepstakes below carefully follow all instructions found elsewhere in this offer.

The **Winners Classic** will award prizes with the following approximate maximum values: 1 Grand Prize: $26,500 (or $25,000 cash alternate); 1 First Prize: $3,000; 5 Second Prizes: $400 each; 35 Third Prizes: $100 each; 1,000 Fourth Prizes: $7.50 each. Total maximum retail value of Winners Classic Sweepstakes is $42,500. Some presentations of this sweepstakes may contain individual entry numbers corresponding to one or more of the aforementioned prize levels. To determine the Winners, individual entry numbers will first be compared with the winning numbers preselected by computer. For winning numbers not returned, prizes will be awarded in random drawings from among all eligible entries received. Prize choices may be offered at various levels. If a winner chooses an automobile prize, all license and registration fees, taxes, destination charges and, other expenses not offered herein are the responsibility of the winner. If a winner chooses a trip, travel must be complete within one year from the time the prize is awarded. Minors must be accompanied by an adult. Travel companion(s) must also sign release of liability. Trips are subject to space and departure availability. Certain black-out dates may apply.

The following applies to the sweepstakes named above:

No purchase necessary. You can also enter the sweepstakes by sending your name and address to: P.O. Box 508, Gibbstown, N.J. 08027. Mail each entry separately. Sweepstakes begins 6/1/93. Entries must be received by 12/30/94. Not responsible for lost, late, damaged, misdirected, illegible or postage due mail. Mechanically reproduced entries are not eligible. All entries become property of the sponsor and will not be returned.

Prize Selection/Validations: Selection of winners will be conducted no later than 5:00 PM on January 28, 1995, by an independent judging organization whose decisions are final. Random drawings will be held at 1211 Avenue of the Americas, New York, N.Y. 10036. Entrants need not be present to win. Odds of winning are determined by total number of entries received. Circulation of this sweepstakes is estimated not to exceed 200 million. All prizes are guaranteed to be awarded and delivered to winners. Winners will be notified by mail and may be required to complete an affidavit of eligibility and release of liability which must be returned within 14 days of date on notification or alternate winners will be selected in a random drawing. Any prize notification letter or any prize returned to a participating sponsor, Bantam Doubleday Dell Publishing Group, Inc., its participating divisions or subsidiaries, or the independent judging organization as undeliverable will be awarded to an alternate winner. Prizes are not transferable. No substitution for prizes except as offered or as may be necessary due to unavailability, in which case a prize of equal or greater value will be awarded. Prizes will be awarded approximately 90 days after the drawing. All taxes are the sole responsibility of the winners. Entry constitutes permission (except where prohibited by law) to use winners' names, hometowns, and likenesses for publicity purposes without further or other compensation. Prizes won by minors will be awarded in the name of parent or legal guardian.

Participation: Sweepstakes open to residents of the United States and Canada, except for the province of Quebec. Sweepstakes sponsored by Bantam Doubleday Dell Publishing Group, Inc., (BDD), 1540 Broadway, New York, NY 10036. Versions of this sweepstakes with different graphics and prize choices will be offered in conjunction with various solicitations or promotions by different subsidiaries and divisions of BDD. Where applicable, winners will have their choice of any prize offered at level won. Employees of BDD, its divisions, subsidiaries, advertising agencies, independent judging organization, and their immediate family members are not eligible.

Canadian residents, in order to win, must first correctly answer a time limited arithmetical skill testing question. Void in Puerto Rico, Quebec and wherever prohibited or restricted by law. Subject to all federal, state, local and provincial laws and regulations. For a list of major prize winners (available after 1/29/95): send a self-addressed, stamped envelope entirely separate from your entry to: Sweepstakes Winners, P.O. Box 517, Gibbstown, NJ 08027. Requests must be received by 12/30/94. DO NOT SEND ANY OTHER CORRESPONDENCE TO THIS P.O. BOX.

SWP 7/93

Don't miss these fabulous
Bantam women's fiction titles

On Sale in August

THE LAST BACHELOR
by Betina Krahn

"One of the genre's most creative writers. Her ingenious romances always entertain and leave readers with a warm glow."—Romantic Times

____56522-2 $5.99/$7.50 in Canada

WICKED PLEASURES
by Penny Vincenzi

The smash British bestseller by the author of Old Sins. "A superior three-star novel. An impressive, silky-smooth saga."—Sunday Telegragh, London

____56374-2 $5.99/not available in Canada

PRINCE OF WOLVES
by Susan Krinard

"...Quite possibly the best first novel of the decade... Susan Krinard has set the standard for today's fantasy romance."—Affaire de Coeur

____56775-6 $4.99/$5.99 in Canada

WHISPERED LIES
by Christy Cohen

For years Leah Shaperson had been trapped in a marriage devoid of passion. Then a stranger's tantalizing touch awakened her desires, and she found that she'd do anything to feel wanted once more. But she would soon learn that the price of forbidden pleasure is steep...

____56786-1 $5.50/$6.99 in Canada

Ask for these books at your local bookstore or use this page to order.

☐ Please send me the books I have checked above. I am enclosing $ _____ (add $2.50 to cover postage and handling). Send check or money order, no cash or C. O. D.'s please.

Name _____

Address _____

City/ State/ Zip _____

Send order to: Bantam Books, Dept. FN145, 2451 S. Wolf Rd., Des Plaines, IL 60018
Allow four to six weeks for delivery.

Prices and availability subject to change without notice.

FN 145 8/94

Bestselling Women's Fiction
Sandra Brown

_____	28951-9 TEXAS! LUCKY	$5.99/6.99 in Canada
_____	28990-X TEXAS! CHASE	$5.99/6.99
_____	29500-4 TEXAS! SAGE	$5.99/6.99
_____	29085-1 22 INDIGO PLACE	$5.99/6.99
_____	29783-X A WHOLE NEW LIGHT	$5.99/6.99
_____	56045-X TEMPERATURES RISING	$5.99/6.99
_____	56274-6 FANTA C	$4.99/5.99
_____	56278-9 LONG TIME COMING	$4.99/5.99

Amanda Quick

_____	28354-5 SEDUCTION	$5.99/6.99
_____	28932-2 SCANDAL	$5.99/6.99
_____	28594-7 SURRENDER	$5.99/6.99
_____	29325-7 RENDEZVOUS	$5.99/6.99
_____	29316-8 RECKLESS	$5.99/6.99
_____	29316-8 RAVISHED	$4.99/5.99
_____	29317-6 DANGEROUS	$5.99/6.99
_____	56506-0 DECEPTION	$5.99/7.50

Nora Roberts

_____	29078-9 GENUINE LIES	$5.99/6.99
_____	28578-5 PUBLIC SECRETS	$5.99/6.99
_____	26461-3 HOT ICE	$5.99/6.99
_____	26574-1 SACRED SINS	$5.99/6.99
_____	27859-2 SWEET REVENGE	$5.99/6.99
_____	27283-7 BRAZEN VIRTUE	$5.99/6.99
_____	29597-7 CARNAL INNOCENCE	$5.50/6.50
_____	29490-3 DIVINE EVIL	$5.99/6.99

Iris Johansen

_____	29871-2 LAST BRIDGE HOME	$4.50/5.50
_____	29604-3 THE GOLDEN BARBARIAN	$4.99/5.99
_____	29244-7 REAP THE WIND	$4.99/5.99
_____	29032-0 STORM WINDS	$4.99/5.99
_____	28855-5 THE WIND DANCER	$4.95/5.95
_____	29968-9 THE TIGER PRINCE	$5.50/6.50
_____	29944-1 THE MAGNIFICENT ROGUE	$5.99/6.99
_____	29945-X BELOVED SCOUNDREL	$5.99/6.99